Mott Abigail, Mary Sutton Wood

Narratives of colored Americans

Printed by order of the Trustees of the residuary estate of Lindley Murray

Mott Abigail, Mary Sutton Wood

Narratives of colored Americans
Printed by order of the Trustees of the residuary estate of Lindley Murray

ISBN/EAN: 9783337185459

Printed in Europe, USA, Canada, Australia, Japan

Cover: Foto ©Andreas Hilbeck / pixelio.de

More available books at **www.hansebooks.com**

NARRATIVES

OF

COLORED AMERICANS.

God "hath made of one blood all nations of men for to
dwell on all the face of the earth."—ACTS xvii., 26.

NEW YORK:
WILLIAM WOOD & CO., 27 GREAT JONES STREET.
1875.

CONTENTS.

PHILLIS WHEATLEY.

In 1761 John Wheatley's wife went to the slave market in Boston, for a girl whom she might train to wait upon her in her old age. At that time ships were sent from Boston to Africa after cargoes of slaves, which were sold to the people of Massachusetts. Among a group of more robust and healthy children just imported from Africa, the lady observed one of slender form, suffering from change of climate and the miseries of the voyage. She was interested in the poor little girl, bought her, and took her home. The child, who was named Phillis, was almost naked, her only covering being a strip of dirty carpet; but in a short time the effects of comfortable clothing and food were visible in her returning health.

Phillis at the time of her purchase was between seven and eight years of age, and the intention of her mistress was to train her as a servant; but the intelligence which the young girl soon exhibited, induced her mistress's daughter to teach her to read. Such was the rapidity with which she learned, that in sixteen months from the time of her arriving in the family, the African child had so mastered the English

1

language, to which she was an utter stranger before, that she could read with ease the most difficult parts of the Bible. Her uncommon intellect altered the intentions of the family regarding Phillis, and she was kept about the person of her mistress, whose affection she won by her amiable disposition and pleasing manners. All her knowledge was obtained without any instruction, except what was given her in the family; and in four years from the time she was stolen from Africa, and when only twelve years of age, she was capable of writing letters to her friends on various subjects.

The young colored girl became an object of very general attention and astonishment; and in a few years she corresponded with several persons in high stations. As she grew up to womanhood, her attainments kept pace with the promise of her earlier years; the literary people of Boston supplied her with books and encouraged her intellectual powers. This was greatly assisted by her mistress, who treated her like a child of the family, admitted her to her own table, and introduced her as an equal to the best society; but Phillis never departed from the humble and unassuming deportment which distinguished her when she stood a little trembling child for sale in the slave market. She respected the prejudice against her color, and, when invited to the tables of the great or wealthy, she chose a place apart for herself, that none might be offended at a thing so unusual as sitting at table with a woman of color.

Such was the modest and amiable disposition of Phillis Wheatley. She studied Latin, and her translations show that she made considerable progress in it; and she wrote poetry. At the age of fourteen she appears to have first attempted literary composition, and by the time she was nineteen the whole of her printed poems appear to have been written. They were published in London in 1773 in a small volume of above 120 pages, containing thirty-nine pieces, which she dedicated to the Countess of Huntington. This work has gone through several editions in England and America.

Most of her poetry has a religious or moral bearing; all breathes a soft and sentimental feeling; many pieces were written on the death of friends. In a poem addressed to a clergyman on the death of his wife, some beautiful lines occur:

> "O come away," her longing spirit cries,
> "And share with me the rapture of the skies.
> Our bliss divine to mortals is unknown,
> Immortal life and glory are our own.
> Here too may the dear pledges of our love
> Arrive, and taste with us the joys above;
> Attune the harp to more than mortal lays,
> And join with us the tribute of their praise
> To Him who died stern justice to atone,
> And make eternal glory all our own."

A poem on the Providence of God contains the following:

"All-wise, Almighty Providence, we trace
  In trees, and plants, and all the flowery race,
  As clear as in the nobler frame of man,
  All lovely ensigns of the Maker's plan.
  The power the same that forms a ray of light,
  That called creation from eternal night."

From a beautiful address and prayer to the Deity:

"Great God, incomprehensible, unknown
  To sense, we bow at thine exalted throne.
  O while we crave thine excellence to feel,
  Thy sacred presence to our hearts reveal,
  And give us of that mercy to partake,
  Which Thou hast promised for the Saviour's sake."

About the twenty-first year of her age Phillis was
liberated; but she continued in her master's family,
where she was much respected. Her health was delicate, and her physician having recommended a sea-
voyage, it was arranged that she should visit England. She had not before been parted from her
adopted mother, and the separation was painful to
both of them.

Phillis was received and admired in the first circles
of English society, her poems published, and her por-
trait engraved. Her countenance appears to have
been pleasing, and her head highly intellectual. The
health of Mrs. Wheatley declined, and she longed for
her beloved companion. On the first notice of her
benefactress's desire to see her, Phillis, whose humility
was not shaken by flattery and attention, re-embarked

for Boston. Within a short time after her return she stood by the dying bed of her mistress, mother, and friend, and Phillis Wheatley found herself alone.

Shortly after the death of her friend she married a respectable man of her own color, named Peters. He was a remarkable person—of good character, a fluent writer, a ready speaker, and altogether an intelligent, educated man. He was a grocer by trade, and, as a lawyer, pleaded the cause of his brethren, the Africans, before the courts. Phillis was twenty-three at the time of her marriage. The connection did not prove a happy one, and she being of a susceptible mind and delicate constitution, fell into a decline, and died in 1780, about the twenty-sixth year of her age.

DELIVERANCE OF A HOTTENTOT FROM A LION.

A METHODIST missionary named Kay, relates the following occurrence :

I visited a poor sick Hottentot in the south of Africa, who recently experienced one of the most remarkable and providential deliverances I ever heard of. I found him in great pain, from the wounds he had received on that occasion. He gave me a description of his escape from the jaws of a lion, which he ascribes wholly to the gracious interposition of the Father of mercies.

1*

About a month ago he went on a hunting excursion, accompanied by several other natives. On an extensive plain they found an abundance of game, and discovered a number of lions, who appeared to be disturbed by their approach. A very large male lion began slowly to advance towards the party, many of whom were young and unaccustomed to such formidable animals. They all dismounted and prepared to fire, and, according to custom, began to tie their horses together by the bridles, with a view to keep them between themselves and the lion until they were able to take deliberate aim.

Before the horses were properly fastened, the monster made a tremendous bound or two, and suddenly pounced upon the hind part of one of the horses, which plunged forward and knocked down the poor Hottentot. His comrades took flight, and ran off with all speed. He rose as quickly as possible to follow them ; but no sooner had he regained his feet than the majestic beast stretched forth his paw, and, striking him behind the neck, brought him to the ground again. He then rolled on his back, and the lion set his foot upon his breast, and lay down upon him. The poor man now became almost breathless, partly from fear, but principally from the pressure of his terrific load. He moved a little to gain air, but, feeling this, the lion seized his left arm, close to the elbow, and amused himself with the limb for some time, biting it in different places, down to the hand. .

All this time the lion did not seem to be angry,

but merely caught at the arm as a cat sports with a mouse that is not quite dead, so that there was not a single bone broken, as there would have been if the lion had been hungry or irritated. While in great agony, and expecting every moment to be torn limb from limb, the sufferer cried to his companions for assistance, but cried in vain. On raising his head a little, the beast opened his dreadful jaws to receive it, but his hat only was rent, and points of the teeth only grazed his skull. The lion set his foot on the arm from which the blood was freely flowing, his paw was soon covered therewith, and he again and again licked it clean, and, with flaming eyes, appeared half inclined to devour the man.

"At this critical moment," said the poor victim, " I recollected having heard that there is a God in heaven who is able to deliver at the last extremity, and I began to pray that He would save me, and not allow the lion to eat my flesh." While the Hottentot was thus engaged in calling on God, the animal turned himself completely round. On perceiving this, the man attempted to get from under him, but the lion became aware of his intention, and laid terrible hold of his right thigh, which gave excruciating pain. He again sent up his cry to God for help, nor were his prayers in vain. The huge creature rose from his seat, and walked majestically off about thirty or forty paces, and then lay down on the grass as if to watch his victim, who ventured to sit up, which attracted the lion's attention; he made no attack, but rose, took his departure, and was seen no more. The man soon arose, took up his gun, and hastened to his terrified companions, who had given him up for dead. He was set upon a horse, and taken to the place where I found him.

Dr. Gambier hastened to his relief, and thought the appearance of the wounds so alarming that amputation of the arm was absolutely necessary. To this, however, the man would not consent, as he had a number of young children, whose subsistence depended on his labor. "As the Almighty has delivered me," said he, "from that horrid death, surely He is able to save my arm also." Astonishing to relate, his wounds are healed, and there is now hope of his ultimate recovery.

ANSWER TO PRAYER.

" I WELL remember," said the son of a Christian missionary, " hearing my mother speak in touching terms of the narrow escapes my father had during our sojourn in Jamaica. He endured five attacks of yellow fever, and on one occasion suffered so much that the medical attendant gave up all hopes of his recovery. For some time he lingered in a state of insensibility hardly to be described. My mother watched and wept; friends did the same; the faithful Christian colored people also wept as they saw life ebbing away. Death seemed just about to seize his prey.

"Prayer-meetings were held, and at last some hundreds of negroes were assembled, earnestly beseeching Almighty God with tears to spare the life of their beloved missionary. Often had he stood up before judges in their defence. Often had he been cast into prison for protecting them from their tyrannical oppressors; and now, with a warmth of affection and intensity of feeling unknown amongst Christians in England, they cried mightily to God. Hour after hour passed by; messengers were passing from the chapel to the mission-house to obtain tidings of the sick man. At length, when his spirit appeared about to depart and to leave all earthly scenes, the pious negroes agreed to unite *silently* in one heartfelt petition to Him ' in whose hand our breath is;' and believing that ' man doth not live by bread only, but by every word that proceedeth out of the mouth of the Lord,' they thus silently, unitedly prayed. The multitude joined in one petition, ascending from their inmost souls; and at that very hour the shadow of death was removed at the rebuke of the Lord !

"A change took place, signs of health appeared, and he for whom so many supplicants prayed was raised up from his bed of languishing, and that chapel did indeed become filled with songs of joy, praise, and thanksgiving. ' He lives! he lives ! ' was the joyful exclamation that ran from one to another through that congregation."

FALLACIES RESPECTING THE RACE OF HAM.

IT is thought by some that the race of Ham, one of the sons of Noah, had a curse pronounced upon it at the beginning, whereby through all time this particular branch of the human family was to be kept in an inferior and servile condition. This is not correct. No curse stands recorded in the Bible against the race of Ham. The curse in question was pronounced upon Canaan, one of the four sons of Ham, whose descendants settled in the hill country, called after his name, along the east end of the Mediterranean Sea. There they dwelt for several centuries, and built up a corrupt and idolatrous nation, until they were dispossessed of their inheritance by the invading hosts of the Jews. By this invasion vast numbers of this Canaanitish race perished, and those who survived were brought into an abject, dependant, and servile condition.

The perversion of the passage is the more noteworthy from the fact, that while Ham was the offender, on account of whose conduct the curse was pronounced—so that the reader is naturally looking for some manifestation towards him personally—his name does not appear. The curse, though three times repeated, falls steadily upon Canaan, one of the four sons. When the three sons of Noah came forth with their father out of the ark, the historian simply says,

"And Ham is the father of Canaan." True, so he was, and was also the father of Misraim, and Cush, and Phut. Shem, too, was the father of five sons, and Japheth of seven; but nothing is said at that time about all these, only, "Ham is the father of Canaan." And so also when Ham's irreverent wickedness is mentioned, it is "Ham the father of Canaan."

What is perhaps still more noticeable, when the curse is passed, and the historian in the next chapter takes up the genealogy of the race after the flood, and shows us the first founders of kingdoms and nations, the only instance in all that long list, when he stops to give us the boundaries of any people, is in this case of Canaan. It seems as if God took especial pains to set the people who were to be cursed, apart from the rest, that there need be no doubt who they were, and where they lived.

But if we take the race of Ham generally, we shall find that for two thousand years after the flood it continued by far the most noticeable and conspicuous of the three branches. For some reason the early developments of civilization were almost entirely in this race. Egypt and Assyria, by far the grandest empires of antiquity, were both of this Hametic order. Misraim, the son of Ham, is the reputed father of the one, and Nimrod, the grandson, of the other. So obvious was this fact, at least as respects Egypt, that it is familiarly called in the Scriptures "the land of Ham." "Israel also came into Egypt, and Jacob sojourned in the land of Ham." And again, "He sent Moses His servant, and Aaron whom He had chosen. They showed His signs among them, and wonders in the land of Ham."

OLD DINAH.

DINAH was a slave. Her mistress was an Indian woman, into whose dark mind not a single ray of gospel light had ever penetrated. She lived among a small tribe on the borders of Tennessee, and although at the age of forty, or a little over, she was called Old Dinah. The Indian mistress and all her servants had been baptized by a Roman priest; but why, or wherefore, none of them knew. Dinah said, in relating the circumstance, "I allers thought the white folks had something to tell that we did not know about, and I used to think what could it be. When the missionaries come here with the Bible, then I know what it is."

Her veneration for the "Good Book," as she always called it, was remarkable. Getting on a stool in her little cabin one day, I noticed on a shelf, far above the reach of her little ones, a pile of torn, dingy bits of paper. I said, "What have you here, Dinah?"

"Oh, missus, don't mind *them* now. I picks 'em up when I come from the meeting. I spose the children throws 'em out of the school-house, but I thinks it may be they are pieces of the Good Book, and when I learns to read I can find 'em out."

Dinah did learn to read. She had a family to provide for, and Saturday was the only day in the week allotted to her in which to look after her little patch of corn and potatoes, cook their food, and prepare her children for the Sabbath. The morning she gave to her farming in summer, then the washing and mending, and at night after the children were washed and stowed away for sleep, she would take the youngest on her back, and, tired as she often was, trudge away two miles to the mission station; and favored indeed was the teacher who could get rid of the earnest appeal, "Let me learn just a little more," before the morning dawned. Every Sabbath morning a little time was spent in imparting to her Daniel the lesson of the previous evening—his master living in a village some miles distant, so that he could not secure any other instruction; but Daniel soon outran his teacher, and having a warm Christian heart, learned to expound as well as read the Good Book, much to the edification of his colored friends. This was also an unfailing source of comfort and grateful recollection to Dinah. Once when listening to his fervent appeals, she said to me, while the big tears chased each other joyously down her cheeks, " Oh, missus, look at Daniel! I taught that man his a, b, c, and now he knows so much, and I can only pick out a little of the Good Book yet."

In the preaching of the gospel she took great delight, and never but once, during our nine or ten months among that people, do I remember her being

absent from our' meetings on the Sabbath. It was
in the female prayer-meeting that Dinah was invaluable. Here all her tenderness of conscience, her desire for instruction, her delicacy and tact in eliciting
it, not only for herself but for the benefit of others
whose spiritual wants she had made her study, and
above all, her meek and earnest supplications, rendered her a helper never to be forgotten, and I loved her
for the image of my Master shining in her face.

"NO-ACCOUNT JOHNNY."

BY M. E. SANGSTER.

"No-Account Johnny" had had a hard time all
his life. He was a poor boy, so homely, and dirty, and
ragged, so nearly idiotic, that few people would look
at him twice. He lived with a French dyer, who had
taught him how to stir the vats at a certain time every
day, and who gave him in return enough corn-bread
and bacon to keep him alive. A damp, ill-smelling
cellar was the place where he spent his days, and his
nights were passed in an equally repulsive attic. To
dodge a blow, to tell a lie, to eat, to sleep, to be glad
in a vague sort of way when the sun shone on him
warmly, these were all the accomplishments of poor
"No-Account Johnny" Long.

Christmas, with its green boughs and its gifts,

went by, and brought no gift to him. He did wish, as he heard the other boys tooting away on their tin horns, that he had one ; but as he could not get one by wishing, he contented himself with turning somersaults on the pavement. By an unfortunate miscalculation, he lay bruised and unconscious at the foot of the cellar-steps.

Aunt Lizzie, the washerwoman, at the end of the court, took him home to her poor little house, and took care of him till he was well again, for in the fall he had broken his arm. Her children went to Sunday-school, and one of them brought his teacher to see Johnny.

"Well, my poor little fellow," said the gentleman, looking with pity on the thin face, clean now, through Aunt Lizzie's care, "I see you are sick ; what's your name ? "

" No-Account Johnny ! "

" Johnny ! well, Johnny, do you know that Jesus loves you ? "

"Never hearn tell of the Mister, I'm no account. Reckon He don't know me ! Missis says I'm no account nohow ! "

" But that is a mistake, my boy. You are of great account. You have a soul that can never die. Did you never know that ? "

" No," shaking his head ; " I don't un'erstand, Mister."

" Was anybody ever good to you, Johnny ? "

" Nobody but Aunt Liz. Aunt Liz been good."

" Well, Jesus is better than Aunt Liz. Jesus is God. He died for you! He lives up there among the stars! He loves you, poor No-Account Johnny. Think of that."

The teacher went away. At the door old Aunt Lizzie thanked him for coming, but said :

" It's of no use, sir, to teach that boy. He a'nt right here," tapping her forehead.

" Ah! Aunt Lizzie, our blessed Jesus can make him understand," said Mr. Allen, as he went away.

After a few weeks Johnny was able to go back to the dyeing establishment. The first Sabbath after, however, he lost his place, for he refused to work, and astonished his master by saying that he was going to Sunday-school. Thither he went, and walking up to Mr. Allen said:

" Here I am! Tell me more 'bout Jesus; I've found out a heap since you told me 'bout Him, and I'm going to be Jesus Christ's Johnny now. No-Account Johnny's gone off altogether."

Nobody could tell how it happened, but that magic word, " Jesus," had done wonders for the little heathen. " He loves me," he had said to himself again and again, and then he had listened, with that unlocked heart, to every word he heard about Jesus, and had learned a great deal. " No-Account Johnny " became one of the best scholars in the little mission-school.

ZACHARY AND THE BOY.

ZACHARY was an Indian of the Mohegan tribe, and belonged to the royal family of his people. He was one of the best of hunters, never returning empty-handed from the chase. But he was a poor, miserable drunkard. He had learned from the white man how to drink " fire-water," and had become so fond of it that he was drunk nearly all the time when he was not hunting. When he had reached the age of fifty years, several of his superiors in the tribe died, leaving only one person between him and the position of chief.

One day Zachary was returning from hunting, and while on his way began to think of his past life and of his future prospects. " What a fool I have been," said he to himself, " having lived so long to act so foolishly. How can such a drunken wretch as I ever hope to be the chief of my tribe? What will my people think and say of me? I am not worthy to fill the place of the great Uncas. I will drink no more ! "

When he reached his wigwam, he told his wife and friends that he would never, as long as he lived, taste any drink but water. And he kept this resolution to the day of his death.

Many of the whites who heard this story could not believe it. They said Zachary had been so long in the habit of drinking that he could not live without it, and they had no doubt that he often took a glass

slyly when no óne was looking on. Among these
was a young man, the son of the governor of one of
the New England colonies; for this story I am telling you is about matters which took place many years
ago, before America was a separate nation, and when
what are now States were called colonies, and gov-
erned by rulers sent over from England.

Zachary had by this time become the chief in his
tribe, and the governor invited him one day to dine
with him. While they were seated at the table the
governor's son thought he would try the temperance
principles of the old chief, and offering him a glass
of beer, said : "Zachary, this beer is excellent, will
you taste it?"

The old man dropped his knife and fork, and leaning over the table, looked with a sharp eye upon the
youth, and said : "John, you do not know what you
are doing! Boy, you are serving the devil! Do
you want to make me what I once was, a poor, miserable man, unfit to govern my tribe? John, the
acorn grows into an oak; the cub becomes a bear;
the brook swells into a river; and a single spark of
fire will spread through a whole forest. So one drop
of your beer would make me want more, and then I
should want something stronger, and I would drink
rum until I became as wretched as I once was. Do
you not know that I am an Indian? I tell you that
I am; and that if I begin to drink beer I cannot stop
without tasting rum. *John, while you live, never
again tempt a man to break a good resolution.*"

The young man knew not what to say. He felt that he had done a mean thing in trying to get old Zachary to break his pledge. His parents were deeply affected at the scene, and often reminded their son of it afterward, charging him never to forget it; and he did not. For years after the Indian chief died, John made frequent visits to his grave, repeating to himself the valuable lesson·he had learned, never to tempt a man to break a good resolution.

Men, and children too, who are trying to become better, ought to be helped, not hindered. Kind words and kind deeds will greatly encourage them ; but to frown upon them, to sneer at them, or to make sport of them, is often a sure way of making them as bad as ever.— *The Christian.*

TRUST IN PROVIDENCE.

ON a bridge I was standing one morning,
    And watching the current roll by,
When suddenly into the water
    There fell an unfortunate fly.

The fishes that swam to the surface,
    Were looking for something to eat,
And I thought that the hapless young insect
    Would surely afford them a treat.

" Poor thing," I exclaimed with compassion,
    " Thy trials and dangers abound,
For if thou escap'st being eaten,
    Thou canst not escape being drowned."

No sooner 'the sentence was spoken,
  Than lo, like an angel of love,
I saw, to the waters beneath me,
  A leaflet descend from above.

It glided serene on the streamlet,
  'Twas an ark to the poor little fly ;
Which, soon to the land reascending,
  Spread its wings to the breezes to dry.

Oh, sweet was the truth that was whispered,
  That mortals should *never* despair,
For He that takes care of an insect,
  Much more for His *children* will care.

And though, to our short-sighted vision,
  No way of escape may appear,
Let us trust, for when least we expect it,
  The help of *our Father* is near.

THE WIFE.

DR. LIVINGSTONE, in his travels in Africa, came one night to the house of Mozinkwa, a friendly man, with a pleasant-looking wife and fine family of children, very "black, but comely." Perhaps their hospitable, kind ways made them look handsome to the lonely missionary, so far from home and friends. He was caught in a heavy rain, but he and his companions received a warm welcome and plenty of food from this friendly couple, till they were able to proceed.

They had a large garden, cultivated by the wife, with yams, sweet potatoes, and other vegetables growing in it, and all surrounded by a fine hedge of the banian tree. Under some larger trees, in the middle of the yard, stood the huts in which they lived, and no doubt the fine-looking little children played many happy days under their mother's care in the shade.

When Dr. Livingstone took his leave of this interesting family, the wife asked him to bring her some cloth from the white man's country. When he returned, after a long journey, he was surprised to find the pleasant home silent and deserted; the garden given up to wild weeds, and the huts in ruins, and no sign of life in the spot where he last saw a large family of frolicking children. Poor *Mozinkwa's wife was dead* and in her grave under the large trees, while the huts, garden, and hedge, of which she had been so proud, were fast going to ruin; for, according to the custom of that heathen country, a man can never continue to live where a favorite wife has died. He is so lonely and sorrowful when he thinks of the happy times they have had together, that he cannot stay where everything reminds him of his loss. If ever he visits the spot again, it is to pray to his dead wife and make some offering. So for want of a knowledge of the Friend of Sinners, who binds up the wounded heart, they must move from place to place, and can never have any settled villages in that part of the country.

How different would the scene have been on Dr.
2

Livingstone's return, if poor Mozinkwa and his wife had been *Christians.* Then he might have been happy even in his loneliness, for he would have prayed to God for strength to bear his loss, and read the Bible, and taught his children to live so as to meet their mother in heaven. Instead of flying from place to place to forget their troubles, those poor Africans might have permanently happy homes, if they knew the peace the gospel gives.

A HOTTENTOT'S LOVE FOR HER TEACH-ERS, AND THE POWER OF PRAYER.

DURING the persecution to which the Moravian missionaries in South Africa were exposed some years ago, a woman, living about an hour's walk from the mission house, had a daughter who attended the school, and had become a Christian. One day this girl returned home in terror, bringing her little sister. Her mother inquired the reason; she replied: "We and our teachers are all to be shot dead, and I have brought my sister back, that you may at least keep one child; but as for me, I will return to my teachers and suffer with them."

"What!" said her mother, "do you mean to go and be killed?"

"Yes," replied the poor girl; "for it is written in the Bible, 'Whoever will lose his life for my sake, shall find it.'"

Her mother was much affected, and taking up her younger daughter, said, "My child, where you are there will I be."

The party then set off for Bavian's Kloof, weeping all the way. When they had arrived at the top of the hill which commanded a view of the settlement, they saw a number of the natives approaching it, as if to attack the missionaries. The Hottentot woman and her children fell upon their knees and cried fervently to God, beseeching Him to prevent the enemy from hurting their beloved teachers. When they again looked up, they saw the men going towards another plantation, at some distance from the mission. The woman and children went to Bavian's Kloof, and found the Hottentots there all in tears, some kneeling, some prostrate on their faces, crying to God, and their most urgent prayers seemed to be, " Preserve the teachers whom Thou hast sent us."

THE LIVING SACRIFICE.

AMID the forest's silent shades
  Where nature reigns supreme,
A little band had met to hear
  The glorious gospel theme.

I gazed upon the dusky forms
  Of Indians gathered there,
And thought how once the red man owned
  Those lands so rich and fair.

But now he roams throughout the plains
  Where once his fathers dwelt,
A poor heart-stricken wanderer,
  For him none pity felt.

But hark ! the preacher's solemn tone
  My wand'ring thoughts recall ;
He preaches Jesus crucified,
  Jesus who died for all.

He tells, with simple eloquence,
  How the Good Shepherd came
To save the erring sheep He loved,
  From ruin and from shame.

He speaks of sad Gethsemane,
  Then tells the eager crowd,
How Jesus Christ was crucified
  By cruel men and proud.

And at his words like forest trees
  Moved by the rushing blast,
O'er the proud hearts of those dark men
  A wondrous change then passed.

They wept—nature's lone children wept
  At that sweet tale of love—
To think that Jesus died that they
  Might dwell with Him above.

And one of that wild forest's sons,
  Of tall and noble frame.
While tears bedewed his manly cheek,
  Towards the preacher came.

" What ? did the blessed Saviour die
And shed His blood for me ?
Was it for *my* sins Jesus wept
In dark Gethsemane ?

" What can poor Indian give to Thee,
Jesus, for love like thine ?
The lands my fathers once possessed
Are now no longer mine ;

" Our hunting-grounds are all upturned
By the proud white man's plough,
My rifle and my dog, alas !
Are my sole riches now.

" Yet these I fain would give to Him
On Calvary's cross who bled ;
Will Christ accept so mean a gift ? "—
The stranger shook his head.

The Indian chief a moment paused,
And downward cast his eyes :
Then suddenly from round his neck
His blanket he unties.

" This, with my rifle and my dog,
Are all I have to give ;
Yet these to Jesus I would bring ;
He died that I might live !

" Stranger ! will Jesus Christ receive
These tokens of my love ? "
The preacher answered, " Gifts like these
Please not the God above."

The humble child of ignorance
　His head in sorrow bent;
Absorbing thought unto his brow
　Its saddening influence lent.

He raised his head, a gleam of hope
　O'er his dark features passed,
As when on some deep streamlet's breast
　The sun's bright beams are cast.

His eyes were filled with glistening tears,
　And earnest was his tone;
"Here is poor Indian! Jesus, take,
　And make him all thine own."

A thrill of joy passed through the crowd,
　To see how grace divine
Could cause the heart of th' Indian chief
　With heav'nly love to shine;—

Such love as made him yield with joy
　Body and soul to Him
Whose watchful care can never fail,
　Whose love can ne'er grow dim.

SAAT.

SIR SAMUEL BAKER and his wife made a dangerous
and toilsome journey into the burning regions of
Central Africa. From a book of travel and adventure
published by him we glean such portions as relate to
their faithful servant, Saat, the African boy.

When a child of six years old, minding his father's goats in the desert, Saat was captured by a hostile Arab tribe, and thrust into a sack, which was placed on a camel's back, and thus he was carried hundreds of miles from home. Every time that the poor child screamed or offered resistance he was threatened that he would be killed by his cruel captors. Saat shortly found himself in the hands of a slave-dealer, by whom he was offered to the Egyptian government as a drummer-boy, but being too small was rejected. A fellow slave told little Saat of an Austrian mission-house in the very town in which they were, that would protect and care for him if he could escape to it. Thither the little boy fled, and found shelter for some time, gaining such instruction as his mind could receive, together with other little waifs and strays, which the missionaries had received at different times.

Sickness reduced the number of the good men who had cared for and taught the children, and they found it necessary to turn adrift the friendless little ones, who apparently without result had been watched and tended, and little Saat, "the one grain of gold," was a second time without a home. But God guided him on a good way.

One evening Sir Samuel Baker and his wife were sitting in their courtyard on the Nile, when a starved, miserable boy crept up to them, and crouching in the dust, begged to be allowed to live with them and be their boy. They did not take him then, and he came again the next day, praying them to allow him to

serve them. They endeavored to discourage him by
telling of the long and dangerous journey they were
about to take. Saat was firm; he would go with
them to the end of the world. Touched by the boy's
story they went to the mission to inquire the truth
of it. There an excellent character was given of
him, with the remark that he must have been turned
out by mistake. This determined the traveller to
adopt him. A good washing and a new suit of
clothes made Saat quite respectable, and being well-
disposed he soon made himself useful. Mrs. Baker
taught him to sew, and Sir Samuel gave him lessons
in shooting. When his day's work was done, he was
allowed to sit by his mistress while she told him
stories from the Bible and from the history of Europe.
There was plenty of time for such talk, the long,
weary journey in the Nile boat, which they had just
commenced, enabling that gentle lady to instruct the
poor ignorant boy thrown on her hands. Their native
servants robbed, betrayed, and deserted the travellers
at every turn, but among them little Saat shone as
a bright star, honest, truthful, and devoted to those
who had rescued him from starvation, and he daily
won their love. To him they most probably owed
their lives, as he detected and exposed to them a
plan their servants had agreed on, to seize their
master's arms and leave him in the desert, or murder
him and his wife if they met with resistance.

This child of the sun seemed to have all the best
points of a happy English boy; he delighted in active

sports and shooting with his light gun. Through dangers and distresses he was always bright and cheerful. Saat was sometimes in mischief, too, and he spoilt two watches by trying to examine their inside works. He was very fond of a drum; but a camel which carried it rolled over and spoilt that musical instrument; then he destroyed a tin kettle and a tin cup by drumming on them. Neither watch nor tinware could be replaced when shops were thousands of miles away. Once, when he was not well, a powder was given him to take, and he asked if he should eat the paper it was in.

Sir Samuel followed his plans for his journey through all obstacles, and Saat's name is never mentioned, except in praise. He endured hunger and thirst, and rejoiced with his kind protectors in the success of their undertaking. During these years of travel, sickness and death had visited their little band, but as yet the boy had been spared; but on the homeward journey his time came,—that fearful sickness, the plague, attacked the vessel in which the party journeyed: first one was smitten, then another, and then it was Saat. Mrs. Baker herself nursed the sick boy with tender care, but he lay day and night in delirium. At last came a calm; he was gently washed and dressed in clean clothes, and laid to rest. He slept; his mistress hoped it was the sleep of recovery; but a kind servant presently covered the boy's face while tears ran down her cheeks. Saat was dead. The boat was stopped, and

2*

the faithful boy was sadly buried beneath a tree, the wonderful river Nile rolling by his grave.

Saat was converted from Paganism to Christianity, and reached his home and rest in heaven.

THE PSALM OF THE SLAVE.

God heard it; and he is free.

LOUD he sang the Psalm of David,
He a negro and enslaved,
Sang of Israel's victory;
Sang of Zion bright and free.

In that hour when night is calmest,
Sang he from the Hebrew Psalmist,
In a voice so sweet and clear,
That I could not choose but hear—

Songs of triumph and ascription,
Such as reached the swarth Egyptian,
When upon the Red-Sea coast
Perished Pharaoh and his host.

And the voice of his devotion,
Filled my soul with strange emotion;
For its tones by turns were glad,
Sweetly solemn, wildly sad.

Paul and Silas in their prison,
Sang of Christ, the Lord arisen;
And an earthquake's arm of might
Broke their dungeon-gates at night.

But, alas ! what holy angel
Brings the slave this glad evangel ?
And what earthquake's arm of night
Breaks his dungeon-gates at night ?

Longfellow.

THE MISSIONARY BOX.

A FEW years ago two young Africans went to
England to obtain an education, and then return to
Africa to teach their countrymen the gospel of Jesus
Christ: One of them, George Nicol, while staying
near London, walked a considerable distance. In
his walk he came to Hampstead Heath, from which
he could see the city of London before him. The
principal buildings attracted his attention. A laborer
who was breaking stones on the other side of the
road, kept looking at him; no doubt it seemed
strange to him to see a colored man looking at the
view he had himself seen every day for many years
past ; and in his eyes, perhaps, the wonder would be
increased by seeing the African dressed like a respectable Englishman.

While George Nicol stood gazing on the scene the
laborer kept peeping at him from time to time, but
never thought of speaking. Presently George Nicol
turned to him, and asked in good English, what a certain building was which he saw in the distance. The
laborer answered civilly that it was St. Paul's Church ;
and then replied to several other questions, till he had

pointed out the chief buildings of the great city, which could be seen from the hill on which they were standing.

When this was done, after a short pause the African said : " Well, my friend, you have here a very large and magnificent city; but, after all, it is not to be compared to the city of God, the heavenly Jerusalem, which I hope you and I will both see one day."

If the honest laborer was surprised before, his astonishment was much greater now.

" Why," said he, " do you know anything about such things ? "

" Yes, thank God," replied the African, " I am happy to say I do. It was not always so. I was once in darkness, and knew nothing of the true God ; but good missionaries from England came, and taught me about Jesus Christ; and now I live in hope of one day seeing Him in that beautiful city, the heavenly Jerusalem, where I shall dwell with Him forever."

By this time the good Englishman had thrown down the hammer with which he had been breaking stones. He came across the road, and grasping Nicol's hand exclaimed, " Why, then, you are one of them that I have been praying for these twenty years. I never put a penny into the missionary box without saying, ' God bless the colored man.' "

It rejoiced the heart of the good African not a little to find in the humble stone-breaker a friend who had taken such a deep interest in the people of Africa.

And if his pleasure was so great, the laborer's was not less, for he saw in George Nicol an answer to his prayers, and a sure proof that his missionary money had not been spent in vain. He felt the truth of the words, " Cast thy bread upon the waters, for thou shalt find it after many days."

HE NEVER TOLD A LIE.

MUNGO PARK, in the account of his African travels, relates that a negro youth was killed by a shot from a party of Moors. His mother walked before the corpse, as it was carried home, frantic with grief, clapping her hands, and declaring her son's good qualities. " He never told a lie," cried the bereaved mother ; " he never told a lie ; no, never."

DADDY DAVY.

ONE winter evening, when a little orphan in my seventh year, I climbed upon my grandfather's knee, and begged that he would " tell me a story." The candles were not yet lighted in the parlor, but the glowing fire sent forth its red blaze, and its cheering heat seemed more grateful from a fall of snow, which was rapidly collecting in piles of fleecy whiteness on the lawn.

I had taken my favorite seat on the evening I have
mentioned, just as a poor negro with scarcely any
covering appeared at the window, and supplicated
charity. His dark skin was deeply contrasted with
the unblemished purity of the falling snow, whilst his
trembling limbs seemed hardly able to support his
shivering frame; and there he stood, perishing in the
land of boasted hospitality and freedom !

With all the active benevolence which my grandfather possessed, he still retained the usual character-
istics of the hardy seaman. He discouraged everything which bore the smallest resemblance to indolence.
The idle vagrant dared not approach his residence ; but
he prized the man of industrious habits, however
lowly his station ; and his influence was ever extended to aid the destitute and to right the injured.

On his first going to sea he had been cabin-boy on
board a Liverpool ship ; he afterwards lived several
years in the island of Trinidad, in the West Indies,
where the slaves were rigorously treated. He there
became well acquainted with the colored people, and
now he no sooner saw the dark face of the poor perishing creature at his window, than he hastily rang
the bell, and a footman entered.

" Robert," said he, " go and bring that poor fellow
in here.''

" Poor fellow, did you say ? " inquired Robert.

" Yes, yes," replied my grandfather, " yonder man,
fetch him here to me."

The servant quitted the room, and it was not with-

out some feelings of fear, as well as hopes of amusement that, a few minutes afterwards, I saw the poor
African stand bowing before the parlor door. The
twilight had faded away, and except the reflection
from the snow, night had thrown its sable shadows
on the scene; but as the bright gleam of the fire shed
its red hue upon the features of the negro, and flashed
upon his rolling eyes, he presented rather a terrific
appearance to my young mind.

" Come in ! " exclaimed my grandfather in a shrill
voice ; but the poor fellow stood hesitatingly on the
border of the carpet till the command was repeated
with more sternness than before, and then the trembling African advanced a few steps towards the easy-
chair in which the veteran was sitting.

Never shall I forget the abject figure which the poor
creature displayed. He was a tall, large-boned man,
but was evidently bent down under the pressure of
sickness and of want rather than of age. A pair of
old canvas trowsers hung loosely on his legs, but his
feet were quite naked. On the upper part of his body
was a striped flannel shirt, one of the sleeves of which
was torn away. He had no covering for his head ;
and the snow which had fallen on it having melted in
the warmth of the room, large, transparent drops of
clear water hung glistening on his thick woolly hair.

His look was inclined downwards, as if fearful of
meeting the stern gaze of my grandfather, who scan-
ned him with the most minute attention, not un-
mingled with agitation. Every joint of the poor

fellow's limbs shook as if struck with ague, and the
cold seemed to have contracted his sinews; for he
crouched his body together, as if to shrink from the
keen blast. Tears were trickling down his cheek, and
his spirit seemed bowed to the earth by distress.

"Tell me," said my grandfather, "what brought
you to England, and what you mean by strolling about
the country here as a beggar? I may order you to
be put in the stocks."

"Ah, massa," replied the negro, "buckra never
have stocks in dis country; yet he die if massa neber
give him something to fill hungry stomach."

While he was speaking my grandfather was restless and impatient. He removed me from his knee,
and looked with more earnestness at the poor man,
who never raised his head. "We have beggars
enough of our own nation," said my grandfather.

"Massa speak true," replied the African, meekly;
"distress live everywhere; come like race-horse, but
go away softly, softly."

Again my grandfather looked sharply at the features
of the man and showed signs of agitation in his own.
"Softly, softly," said he, "that's just your cant. I
I know the whole gang of you, but you are not going
to deceive me; now wouldn't you sacrifice me and
all I am worth for a bunch of plantains?"

"Massa have eat the plantains, den," said the man,
"and yet massa think hard of poor negur who work to
make them grow. God Almighty send rain—God Almighty send sun—but God Almighty send negur too."

" Well, well," said my grandfather, softening his voice, " God is no respecter of colors, and we must not let you starve, daddy; so, Robert, tell the cook to get some warm broth, and bid her bear a hand about it."

" God forever bless massa," exclaimed the poor man, as he listened to the order, and keenly directed his eye towards the person who had issued it; but my grandfather had turned his head toward me, so his face was not seen by the grateful man.

" So I suppose you are some runaway slave ? " said my grandfather, harshly.

" No, massa," rejoined the African, " no, massa ; never run away—I free man. Good buckra give freedom ; but then I lose kind massa, and "——

" Ay, ay," replied my grandfather, " but what about Plantation Joseph, in Trinidad ? "

" Ky ! " responded the man, as his eyes were bent upon his questioner, who again hid his face ; " de buckra knows ebery ting; him like the angel of light to know the secret of the heart."

" Come nearer to the fire, Daddy Davy," said my grandfather, as he bent down to stir the burning coals with the poker.

Never shall I forget the look of the African ; joy, wonder, and admiration were pictured in his face, as he exclaimed, while advancing forward—

" De buckra know my name too !—how dis ? "

My grandfather having kindled a bright flame that illuminated the whole room, turned his face towards

the African ; but no sooner had the poor fellow caught
sight of his features than, throwing himself at his
feet, he clasped the old sailor's knees, exclaiming,
" My own massa!—what for you give Davy him
freedom ? and now do poor negur die for want ! but no,
neber see de day to go dead, now me find my massa."

" Willie, my boy," said my grandfather, turning to
me, " fetch my pocket-handkerchief off the sofa."

I immediately obeyed, but I used the handkerchief
two or three times to wipe the tears from my eyes
before I delivered it to him.

At this moment Robert opened the door, and said
the broth was ready, but stood with amazement to
see the half-naked man at his master's feet.

" Go, Davy," said my grandfather, " go and get
some food ; and, Robert, tell the cook to have a warm
bath ready, and the housemaid must run a pan of
coals over the little bed in the blue room, and put
some extra blankets on. You can sleep without a
nightcap, I dare say, Davy. There, go along, Davy,
go along ; " and the gratified negro left the room with
unfeigned ejaculations of " Gor Amighty for eber bless
kind massa ! "

As soon as the door was closed, and I was once
more seated on my grandfather's knee, he commenced
his usual practice of holding converse with himself.
" What could have brought him here ? " said he. " I
gave him his freedom, and a piece of land to cultivate.
There was a pretty hut upon it, too, with a double
row of cocoa-nut trees in front, and a garden of plan-

tains behind, and a nice plot of guinea-grass for a cow,
and another of buckwheat—what has become of it
all I wonder? Bless me, how time flies! it seems
but the other day that I saved the fellow from a
couple of bullets, and he repaid the debt ·by rescuing
my Betsy—ah, poor dear! She was your mother,
William, and he snatched her from a dreadful and
· terrific fate. How these things crowd upon my mind!
The earthquake shook every building to its foundation
—the ground yawned in horrible deformity, and your
poor mother—we can see her gravestone from the
drawing-room window, you know, for she died since
we have been here, and left her old father's heart a
dreary blank. Yet not so either, my child," pressing
me to his breast and laying his hoary head on mine,
"not so either, for she bequeathed you to my guardian care, and you are now the solace of my gray
hairs."

I afterwards learned that Davy had rescued my
dear mother from destruction, at the risk of his own
life, during an earthquake in Trinidad, for which my
grandfather had given him his freedom, together with
the hut and the land. But he had no protector in
the west: the slaves plundered his property; sickness
came, and no medical attendant would minister to his
wants without the accustomed fee; he contracted
debts, and his ground was sold to the estate on which
it was situated, to pay the lawyers. He quitted the
island of Trinidad to go to Berbice; but, being wrecked near Mahaica Creek, on the east coast of Demer-

ara, he lost his free papers, was seized by the government, and sold as a slave, to pay the expense of ad-
vertising and his keep. He fortunately fell into the
hands of a kind master, who at his death once more
set him at liberty, and he had come to England in the
hope of bettering his condition. But here misfortune
still pursued him : the gentleman whom he accompanied died on the passage ; he could obtain no employment on his landing ; he had been plundered of
what little money he possessed, and had since wandered about the country till the evening that he implored charity and found a home.

My worthy grandfather is now numbered with the
dead ; and I love to sit upon his gravestone at the
evening hour ; it seems as if I were once more placed
upon his knee, and listening to his tales of bygone
years. But Daddy Davy is still in existence, and
living with me. Indeed, whilst I have been writing,
I have had occasion to put several questions to him
on the subject, and he has been fidgeting about the
room to try and ascertain what I was relating respecting him.

"I am only giving a *sketch* of my grandfather,
Davy," said I.

" *Catch*, massa ! what he call *catch ?* "

" About the schooner, and Trinidad, and the earthquake, Davy."

" And da old massa what sleep in de *Werk-en-
rust ?* "

" Yes, Davy, and the snow-storm."

"Ah, da buckra good man! Davy see him noder time up dare," pointing toward the sky. "Gor Amighty for eber bless kind massa!"

AN AGED CHRISTIAN.

"ONE afternoon," writes an American missionary in Africa, "I went to see old Father Scott, an aged dying African. He sent me word he would like to see me. He is in an old dilapidated shanty. A few boards knocked together, raised about a foot from the floor, served as a bedstead. The straw bed we made for him on our first arrival. A little bench, on which were two Bibles and an earthen jar for water, was all the furniture he possessed. He is dependent for food and care on his neighbors, as he is perfectly helpless.

A woman who was near brought me a stool, and I sat down beside him. He was delighted to see me; he told me he had served the Lord for forty years. He had been a Methodist preacher for many years, and had often preached three times a day, though he could never read a word. He would get some boy to read to him several chapters in the Bible, till he got hold of just the text that would suit him. I was very much surprised at his familiarity with the Bible. He could tell me where to find almost any passage.

I could not but look at that poor old man, with his few privileges, and compare them with those of our more favored people. As I looked at him in his penury, witnessed his happiness and his implicit faith, and saw how near home he was, I felt that he was really to be envied. Who can doubt the power of Divine grace? I read to him, and talked to him on the glories of the resurrection, and the mansions our Saviour has prepared for those who love Him; and then I left him with the promise of soon seeing him again. He is almost blind. He begged me not to forget him in my prayers. He is dying of old age, yet no one knows how old he is.

UNCLE JACK:

He was a remarkable African slave of Virginia. It is probable he was brought to James River in the last slave-ship that brought slaves to that State. Such was the regard in which he was held that, on the death of his master, several benevolent persons subscribed a sufficient sum to purchase his freedom.

Uncle Jack's talents were of a high order, and his knowledge of human nature very remarkable. Dr. Rice, of Richmond, said of him, "The old man's acquaintance with the Scriptures is wonderful. Many of his interpretations of obscure passages are singularly just and striking." He spoke pure English. A few anecdotes will convey a good idea of his ready and apt mode of illustration. A person addicted to horse-racing and card-playing, stopped Uncle Jack on the road and said, "Old man, you Christians say a great deal about the way to heaven being narrow. Now if this is so, a great many who profess to be travelling it will not find it half wide enough."

"That's very true," was the reply, "of all that have merely a name to live, and all like you."

"Why refer to me," said the man; "if the road is wide enough for any, it is for me."

"By no means," said Uncle Jack. "You will want to take along a card-table, or a race-horse or two. Now there is no room along this way for such things."

A man who prided himself on his morality said to Uncle Jack: "Old man, I am as good as I need to be. I can't help thinking so, because God blesses me as much as he does you Christians; and I don't know what more I want than He gives me."

To this the old preacher replied, with great seriousness, "Just so with the hogs. I have often looked at them, rooting among the leaves in the woods, and finding just as many acorns as they needed; and yet I never saw one of them look up to the tree from whence the acorns fell."

On one occasion some unruly persons undertook to arrest and whip him, and also several of his hearers, for holding religious meetings. After the arrest one of the men thus accosted Uncle Jack, "Well, old fellow, you are the ringleader of these meetings, and we have been anxious to catch you; now what have you to say for yourself?"

"Nothing at all, master," was the reply.

"What! nothing to say against being whipped! how is that?"

"I have been wondering a long time," said the old Christian, "how it was that so good a man as the Apostle Paul should have been whipped three times for preaching the Gospel, while such an unworthy man as I am should have been 'permitted to preach twenty years without getting a lick." The young men immediately released him.

Uncle Jack died in 1843, aged one hundred years. —*Blake's Biographical Dictionary.*

CHRISTIAN KINDNESS.

In one of my early journeys, says Moffat, with some of my companions, we came to a heathen village on the borders of Orange River, South Africa. We had travelled far, and were hungry, thirsty, and fatigued. From the fear of being exposed to lions, we preferred remaining at the village to proceeding further during the night. The people of the village rather roughly directed us to halt at a distance. We asked for water, but they would not supply it. I offered the three or four buttons which still remained on my jacket for a little milk; this also was refused. We had the prospect of another hungry night at a distance from water, though within sight of the river.

We found it difficult to reconcile ourselves to our lot; for in addition to repeated rebuffs, the manner of the villagers excited suspicion.

When twilight drew on, a woman approached from the height beyond which the village lay. She bore on her head a bundle of wood, and had a vessel of milk in her hand. The latter, without opening her lips, she handed to us, laid down the wood, and returned to the village. A second time she approached with a cooking-vessel on her head, a leg of mutton in one hand, and water in the other. She sat down without saying a word, prepared the fire, and put on the meat. We asked again and again who she was. She remained silent until affectionately entreated to give us a reason for such unlooked-for kindness to strangers. A tear stole down her sable cheek as she replied : " I love Him whose servants you are ; and surely it is my duty to give you a cup of cold water in His name. My heart is full ; therefore I cannot speak the joy I feel to see you in this out-of-the-way place."

On learning a little of her history, we found she was a solitary light burning in a dark place. I asked her how she kept up the life of God in her soul, in the entire absence of the communion of saints. She drew from her bosom a copy of the Dutch New Testament, which she had received from brother Helm when in his school several years since, before she had been compelled by her connections to retire to her present seclusion. " This," she said, " is the fountain whence I drink : this is the oil which makes my lamp burn."

3

I looked on the precious relic, and the reader may imagine how I felt, and my companions with me, when we met with this disciple, and mingled our sympathies and prayers together at the throne of our heavenly Father.

GRATITUDE OF SLAVES.

BY DR. LETTSOM.

DR. LETTSOM was born in the West Indies, and inherited fifty slaves, which was all the property his father left him. He gave freedom to his slaves; and during a long life, with a large practice as a physician in London, he kept up a correspondence with some of those who were indebted to him for their liberty. When he went to the West Indies to settle his father's estate, he made a visit to Tortola, and wrote to a friend as follows:

" I frequently accompanied Major John Pickering to his plantations, and as he passed his numerous negroes saluted him in a loud song, which they continued as long as he remained in sight. I was also a melancholy witness to their attachment to him after his death. He expired suddenly, and when few of his friends were near him. I remember I held his hand when the final period arrived, but he had scarcely breathed his last breath before it was known to his slaves, and instantly about five hundred of them surrounded the house and insisted on seeing their master.

" They commenced a dismal and mournful yell, which was communicated from one plantation to another, till the whole island of Tortola was in agitation, and crowds of negroes were accumulating around us. Distressed as I was by the loss of my relation and friend, I could not be insensible to the danger of a general insurrection; or, if they entered the house, which was constructed of wood, and mounted into his chamber, there was danger of its falling by their weight and crushing us in its ruins.

" In this dilemma I had resolution enough to secure the doors, and thereby prevent sudden intrusion. After this precaution I addressed them through a window, assuring them that if they would enter the house in companies of only twelve at a time, they should all be admitted to see their deceased master, and that the same lenient treatment of them should still be continued. To this they assented, and in a few hours quiet was restored. It affected me to see with what silent, fixed melancholy they departed from the remains of this venerable man."

THE SLAVE SHOEMAKER.

A LADY, who was a Quaker, travelled several years ago through some of the Southern States on a gospel mission. When near the borders of North Carolina, while the horses were being fed, she walked towards a poor hut, and on entering it saw an aged

man engaged in making shoes. He was very black,
but his hair was white and his countenance thoughtful; he looked up surprised, and when she asked if
she might come in and sit down, he replied, " Will
mistress sit with me? " She inquired if he was a
slave, and if he had a wife and children. He said,
" If mistress will hear me I will tell her. I have a
wife and four children, but massa sold them into
Georgia." Wiping his eyes with the sleeve of his
shirt, he continued, " I am a slave, but, mistress, ever
since I got religion God has sweetened my bitter cup,
and made smooth my rough path ; my bitter cup was
parting with my wife and children—my rough path is
slavery."

She asked him how he got religion. He replied,
" My massa let me go to hear preaching, and I remember what the minister said."

" Can thou read ? "

" No, mistress, but God helps me remember ; fourteen years ago I got religion ; I was bad before ;
massa bad too. When I got religion, I was good ;
massa was kind too ; hard things were made easy ;
bitter cups were sweetened. Mistress knows what
that means (looking at her earnestly). I know you
do. Massa gives me work, and I must do it ; nobody comes here, but overseer walks by once a day
to see if I at work ; then the rest of the time is my
own ; I have one and sometimes two hours."

" How does my Christian brother employ his own
time ? " asked the lady.

"I will tell you, mistress: I shut the door, then sit down on that bench and wait upon God; and what good times I have! Sometimes I go to prayer, and God puts words into my mouth; then other times something here (laying his hand upon his breast) tells me not to pray, but to be still—wait upon God in silence; and did my massa and the white people know how good I felt, they would be glad to come and sit with me. In heaven, mistress, God makes no difference—massa and slave all one."

The lady's companions now called for her, and put an end to this very interesting conversation. His parting address was: "Farewell, mistress, till we meet again in heaven. God bless you." With tears they parted.

LET ME RING THE BELL.

A MISSIONARY far away,
　　Beyond the Southern sea,
´ Was sitting in his home one day,
　　With Bible on his knee,

When suddenly he heard a rap
　　Upon the chamber door,
And opening, there stood a boy,
　　Of some ten years or more.

He was a bright and happy child,
　　With cheeks of dusky hue,
And eyes that 'neath their lashes smiled
　　And glittered like the dew.

He held his little form erect,
  In boyish sturdiness,
But on his lip you could detect
  Traces of gentleness.

"Dear sir," he said, in native tongue,
  "I do so want to know,
If something for the house of God
  You'd kindly let me do."

"What can you do, my little boy?"
  The missionary said,
And as he spoke he laid his hand
  Upon the youthful head.

Then bashfully, as if afraid
  His secret wish to tell,
The boy in eager accents said,
  "Oh, let me ring the bell!

"Oh, please to let me ring the bell
  For our dear house of prayer;
I'm sure I'll ring it loud and well,
  And I'll be always there!"

The missionary kindly looked
  Upon that upturned face,
Where hope, and fear, and wistfulness
  United, left their trace.

And gladly did he grant the boon:
  The boy had pleaded well,
And to the eager child he said,'
  "Yes, you shall ring the bell!"

Oh, what a pleased and happy heart
    He carried to his home,
And how impatiently he longed
    For the Sabbath-day to come !

He rang the bell, he went to school,
    The Bible learned to read,
        And in his youthful heart they sowed
    The gospel's precious seed.

And now to other heathen lands
    He's gone, of Christ to tell ;
And yet his first young mission was
    To ring the Sabbath bell.

THE FLIGHT OF A SLAVE.

JAMES —— was born a slave in the State of Maryland. He was so useful as a blacksmith that his value was at least one thousand dollars. He was brought up in total ignorance of letters or of religion, but he always aimed to be trustworthy. He sought to distinguish himself in the finer branches of the business, by invention and finish, making fancy hammers, hatchets, etc. One day his master thought James was watching him improperly, and fell into a panic of rage. "He came down upon me with his cane," said James, "and laid over my shoulders, arms, and legs about a dozen severe blows, so that my flesh was sore for several weeks." He felt the

disgrace of the beating so acutely that he determined
to abscond, and if possible reach the free soil of
Pennsylvania.

One Sunday night, in November, he stole away
into the woods, with only half a pound of Indian
corn-bread to sustain him on his journey, which
would take several days. At three o'clock in the
morning his strength began to fail, his scanty supply
of food afforded poor nourishment, and the only
shelter he could find, without risking travelling by
daylight, was a corn-shock but a few hundred yards
from the road, and there he passed his first day out.
As night came on he pursued his journey; it was
cloudy, and he could not see the north star, which
was his only guide to freedom. His bread was all
eaten, he felt his strength failing, and his mind was
filled with melancholy.   •

In this condition he travelled all the night, and
just at the dawn of day he found a few sour apples,
and took shelter under the arch of a bridge, where he
lay in ambush through the day. Night came on, and
he once more proceeded on his wearisome journey.
Frequently he was overcome with hunger and fatigue, and sat down and slept a few minutes. At
dawn of day he saw a toll-bar, and here he ventured
to ask the best way to Philadelphia, and set off in
the right direction. His taking the open road was
fatal. He was observed by a man, and ordered to
give an account of himself. After a parley, James
took to his heels; but a hue and cry being raised he

was speedily captured. Led to a tavern as a prisoner, he was questioned. He persisted in saying he
was a free man, but he had no free papers. Though
his story was false, we must remember that he knew
not the wickedness of a lie, for he knew nothing of
God and our Saviour.

Toward night, being watched only by a boy, he
contrived to slip away, and again took to the woods.

Wandering in darkness, the north star being covered with clouds, he was at a loss as to what course
to pursue. " At a venture," says he, " I struck
northward in search of a road. After several hours
of laborious travel, dragging through briers and
thorns, I emerged from the woods and found myself
wading through marshy ground and over ditches, and
came to a road about three o'clock in the morning.

" It so happened I came where there was a fork in
the road of three prongs. Which was the right one
for me ? After a few moments' parley with myself, I
took the central prong of the road, and pushed on
with all my speed. It had not cleared off, but a
fresh wind had sprung up; it was chilly and search-
ing. This, with my wet clothes, made me very uncomfortable."

He saw a farm with a small hovel-like barn; into
this he went and buried himself in the straw. Here
he lay the whole day; his only danger was from the
yelping of a small dog, and the noise of horsemen who
passed in search of him. He heard them say they
were after a runaway negro, who was a blacksmith,
3*

and that a reward of two hundred dollars was offered for his recovery. Night came, and he was again on his way, but all he could do was to keep his legs in motion. There came a heavy frost, and he expected every moment to fall to the ground and perish.

Coming to a corn-field covered with heavy shocks of corn, he gathered an ear and then crept into one of the shocks ; he ate as much as he could, expecting to travel on, but fell asleep, and when he awoke the sun was shining. He was obliged to conceal himself as well as he could through the day ; he began again to eat the hard corn, and it took all the forenoon to eat his breakfast. Night came, and he sallied out, feeling much better for the corn he had eaten.

He now believed himself near to Pennsylvania, and under this impression, skipped and danced for joy. He says : " A little after the sun rose I came in sight of a toll-gate ; for a moment I felt some hesitation, but on arriving at the gate I found it attended by only an elderly woman, whom I afterwards heard was a widow and an excellent Christian. I asked her if I was in Pennsylvania. On being informed that I was, I asked if she knew where I could get employment. She said she did not, but advised me to go to W. W., a Quaker, who lived about three miles from her, and whom I would find to take an interest in me. In about half an hour I stood at the door of W. W. After knocking, the door opened upon a comfortably spread table. Not daring to enter, I said I had been sent to him in search of employment.

"'Well,' said he, 'come in, and take thy breakfast and get warm.'

"These words made me feel, in spite of all my fear and timidity, that I had, in the providence of God, found a friend and a home. He at once gained my confidence, and from that day to this, whenever I discover the least disposition in my heart to disregard poor and wretched persons with whom I meet, I call to mind these words: 'Come in, and take thy breakfast and get warm.'

"I was a starving fugitive, without home or friends, and no claim upon him to whose door I went. Had he turned me away I must have perished. Nay, he took me in, and gave of his food, and shared with me his own garments."

By W. W. the wretched wanderer was fed, clothed, and employed, and not only so, but he was instructed in reading, writing, and much useful knowledge. Here, for the first time, did he learn one word of the truths of religion.

James resided with the benevolent Quaker for six months, when it became necessary for him to depart and go elsewhere. He found employment on Long Island, opposite New York. By the kindness of his friends he was educated, and became a Christian minister and pastor of a colored congregation in connection with the Presbyterian Church.

BENJAMIN BANNEKER.

HE was born in Baltimore County, Maryland, in the year 1732. There was not a drop of white man's blood in his veins. His father was born in Africa, and his mother's parents were both natives of Africa. What genius he had must be credited to that race. Benjamin's mother was a remarkable woman. Her name was Morton before marriage, and her nephew, Greenbury Morton, was gifted with a lively and impetuous eloquence which made its mark in his neighborhood. Her husband was a slave when she married him, but she soon purchased his freedom. Together they bought a farm of two hundred acres, which though but ten miles from Jones' Falls, was at that time a wilderness.

When Benjamin was approaching manhood he attended an obscure country school, where he learned reading and writing, and a little arithmetic. Beyond these rudiments he was entirely his own teacher.

Perhaps the first wonder among his neighbors was when, at thirty years of age, he made a clock. It is probable that this was the first clock of which every portion was made in America. He had seen a watch, but never a clock ; and it was as purely his own invention as if none had ever been made before.

The clock attracted the attention of the Ellicott family, well educated men, and Quakers. They gave him books and astronomical instruments. From this time astromony became the great object of Benjamin's life. He remained unmarried, and lived in a cabin on the farm his father left him; he still labored for a living, but his wants were few and simple. He slept much in the day, that he might observe at night-the heavenly bodies, whose laws he was studying. The first almanac prepared by Banneker was for the year 1792, when he was fifty-nine years old, and he continued to prepare almanacs till 1802.

He had become known and respected by scientific men, and received tokens of regard from many of them. The Commissioners to run the lines of the District of Columbia invited Banneker to assist them, and treated him in all respects as an equal.

A gentleman writes of Banneker: "When I was a boy I became very much interested in him, as his manners were those of a perfect gentleman—kind, generous, hospitable, humane, dignified, and pleasing--and he abounded in information on all the various subjects of the day." His head was covered with thick white hair, which gave him a dignified and venerable appearance. His dress was uniformly of superfine drab broadcloth, made with straight collar, a long waistcoat, and broad-brimmed hat. In size and personal appearance the statue of Franklin, in the Library of Philadelphia, as seen from the street, is a perfect likeness of him.

REPENTANCE AND AMENDMENT IN A COLORED SCHOOL AT CHRISTIANSBURG.

Two days since, one of my boys had been behaving badly all the afternoon. I think I spoke to him three times during the session, and it seemed to have no effect; so when five o'clock came, I told him I would see him after school. When the other scholars had left, I went and sat down by him, and talked to him a short time. Among other things, I told him that I could not teach a boy who would do so badly, and that I wanted him to kneel down with me, and I would ask the Lord to watch over him after I had to give him up. He was crying very hard, and we knelt down together. When I came to that part of my prayer, he screamed out, "O Lord! don't let Miss Lucy turn me out of school. *Please*, Lord, don't let her! I know I have been a bad boy, but I won't do so any more. Oh! help her to forgive me. O Jesus! I love to come to school! do forgive me for being so wicked!" Of course I forgave him. He has given me no trouble since, and I do not think he will. —*Am. Freedman.*

AN INCIDENT.

DURING the late rebellion the Confederate army burnt the town of Hampton, Va., as they left it, to prevent the Union troops, who were approaching, taking possession of the houses for winter-quarters. Soon afterwards a gentlemen was riding through the deserted streets and heard the voices of children, but saw no one ; all the white inhabitants of the town had fled with the Confederate army, and the colored people were employed around the camp beyond the town. He stopped his horse and listened, then advanced in the direction from which the voices seemed to come, and looked within the four blackened walls and half-burnt wood-work of what had been a lordly mansion. There he saw forty colored children seated on heaps of stones and charred wood, rejoicing and singing "The Christian's Home." They added the last verse.

I have a home above,
From sin and sorrow free ;
A mansion which eternal love
Design'd and form'd for me.

My Father's gracious hand
Has built this sweet abode,
From everlasting it was plann'd,
My dwelling-place with God.

My Saviour's precious blood
Has made my title sure ;
He passed through death's dark raging flood
To make my rest secure.

The Comforter is come,
The Earnest has been given ;
He leads me onward to the home
Reserv'd for me in heaven.

Bright angels guard my way ;
His ministers of power
Encamping round me night and day,
 Preserve in danger's hour.

Lov'd ones are gone before,
 Whose pilgrim days are done ;
I soon shall greet them on that shore,
 Where partings are unknown.

But more than all I long
 HIS glories to behold,
Whose smile fills all that radiant throng,
 With ecstasy untold.

That bright, yet tender smile
 (My sweetest welcome there),
Shall cheer me through the little while
 I tarry for Him here.

Thy love, thou precious Lord,
 My joy and strength shall be ;
Till Thou shalt speak the glad'ning word
 That bids me rise to Thee.

And then through endless days,
 Where all Thy glories shine,
In happier, holier strains I'll praise
 The grace that made me Thine.

Before the great *I AM*,
 Around His throne above,
The song of Moses and the Lamb,
 We'll sing with deathless love.

There is no sorrow there !
There is no sorrow there !
In heaven above where all is love,
There is no sorrow there.

SOJOURNER TRUTH.

A MAN and his wife and their children were brought from Africa to America, and were sold as slaves. One little girl and her mother kept together, but the others were so far separated that they never met again. The little girl's name was Isabella ; but when she grew to be a woman and became a Christian, she adopted the name of Sojourner Truth.

She told a lady, "I can remember, when I was a little thing, how my ole mammy would sit out of doors in the evenin', an' look up at the stars an' groan. She'd groan, an' groan, and says I to her :

" 'Mammy, what makes you groan so ? '

" An' she'd say, 'Matter enough, chile ! I'm groaning to think of my poor children ; they dou't know where I be, and I don't know where they be ; they looks up at the stars, an' I looks up at the stars, but I can't tell where they be.'

" 'Now,' she said, 'chile, when you be grown up, you may be sold away from your mother an' all your ole friends, an' have great troubles come on ye ; an' when you has these troubles come on ye, ye jes go to God, an' He'll help ye.' "

Isabella was sold to a hard master and mistress.
3

She thought she had got into trouble, and she wanted
to find God; she prayed that He would make her
master and mistress better, and as He did not do so,
she concluded they were too bad to be made better,
and that she might leave them. So she rose at three
o'clock one morning, and travelled till late at night,
when she came to a house and went in, "And," she
said, "they were Quakers, an' real kind they was to
me. They jes took me in, an' did for me as kind as
ef I had been one of 'em, an' I stayed an' lived with
'em two or three years. An' now, jes look here; instead o' keeping my promise an' being good, as I told
the Lord I would, jest as soon as everything got agoing
easy, I forgot all about God, an' I gin up praying."

Sojourner did not long continue in this dark state,
but she found the Lord Jesus, and she said, "I shouted
and cried, Praise, praise, praise to the Lord; an' I
began to feel such a love in my soul as I never felt
before,—love to all creatures. An' then all of a sudden it stopped; an' I said, 'There are the white folks,
that have abused you, an' beat you, an' abused your
people,—think o' them!' An' then there came
another rush o' love through my soul, an' I cried out
loud, 'Lord, Lord, 1 can love even the white folks.
Jesus loved me! I knowed it, I felt it.'"

When slavery was abolished in the State of New
York, Sojourner went back to her old mistress and
demanded her son; he had been sent to Alabama.
After some trouble and expense her son was brought
back to her, though her mistress said to her:

"What a fuss you make about a little nigger ! got more of 'em now than you know what to do with."

" Sojourner," said a gentleman, "you seem to be very sure about heaven."

"Well, I be ; " she answered triumphantly.

" What makes you so sure there is any heaven ? "

" Well, because I got such a hankering arter it in here," she said, giving a thump on her breast with her usual energy.

" Sojourner, did you always go by this name ? "

" No, 'deed ! My name was Isabella. No, 'deed ! but when I left the house of bondage, I left everything behind. I want goin' to keep nothin' of Egypt about me, and so I went to the Lord and asked him to give me a new name. And the Lord gave me Sojourner, because I was to travel up an' down the land, showing the people their sins, an' being a sign unto them. Afterwards I told the Lord I wanted another name, 'cause everybody else had two names ; and the Lord gave me *Truth*, cause I was to declare the truth to the people."

Wendell Phillips relates a scene of which he was witness before the abolition of slavery in the United States. It was in a crowded public meeting in Faneuil Hall, Boston, where Frederick Douglas was one of the chief speakers. Douglas had been describing the wrongs of the colored race, and as he proceeded he grew more and more excited, and finally ended by saying that they had no hope of justice from the whites, no possible hope except in their own right

arms. It must come to blood; they must fight for
themselves, or it would never be done.

Sojourner was sitting, tall and dark, on the very
front seat facing the platform; and in the hush of
feeling after Frederick sat down, she spoke out in her
deep peculiar voice, heard all over the house:

"Frederick, *is God dead?*"

The effect was perfectly electrical, and thrilled
through the whole house, changing as by a flash, the
whole feeling of the audience. Not another word she
said or needed to say, it was enough.

The following is from a letter from a lady who
visited Freedman's Village, near Washington, where
Sojourner Truth was residing in a little frame building with the American flag over the door.

"We found Sojourner Truth, tall, dark, very
homely, but with an expression of determination and
good sense by no means common. She apologized for
her hoarseness, as she had a meeting last evening.
We asked what she had been doing there. 'Fighting
the devil,' she said. What particular devil? 'An
unfaithful man who has undertaken work for which
he is not competent. My people,' she added, 'have
fallen very low, and no one need take hold to help
raise them up as a matter of business, it must be done
from love.' She greatly complained of some one who
had an office in relation to the Freedmen, and said he
ought to be removed. She was asked why she did
not go to the President with her story of the wrong-

doing. She said, ' Don't you see the President has a big job on hand? Any little matter Sojourner can do for herself she aint going to bother him with.' "

KATY FERGUSON;

OR, WHAT A POOR COLORED WOMAN MAY DO.

ABOUT the year 1774, Katy Ferguson was born. Her mother was a slave, and was taken from her young child and sold to another master.

Uneducated and unaided in her parental duties, this poor Christian mother had been faithful to the extent of her abilities, and left upon the mind of her child indelible religious impressions. Katy, in speaking of this cruel separation, many years afterward, said : " Mr. B. sold my mother, and she was carried away from me ; but I remember that before they tore us asunder, she kneeled down, laid her hand upon my head, and gave me to God."

Katy's active mind sought every opportunity of acquiring knowledge. Her mother had taught her much that she herself remembered of the Scriptures. Other persons had taught her the catechism, and · her retentive memory seldom lost what had been committed to it.

In her fifteenth year, the Holy Spirit applied to her conscience and heart the truths of Scripture which

she had thus received. But when awakened to a
perception of her sinfulness, she felt the need of some
kind counsellor.

Neither master nor mistress had ever encouraged
her to communicate her thoughts on religious subjects. The minister on whose services she attended,
Dr. John M. Mason, was a man of such a command-
ing figure and bearing as to inspire her with fear,
rather than confidence. Yet she knew he was a faithful servant of Christ, and that he would care for her
soul. She accordingly ventured to call on him. She
remarked afterward, " While I was standing at the
door, after having rung the bell, my feelings were indescribable. And when the door was opened, and I
found myself in the minister's presence, I trembled
from head to foot. One harsh word or look would
have crushed me." But this faithful minister of
Christ at once appreciated her solicitude, and in the
gentlest manner inquired, " Have you come here to
talk with me about your soul? " This kind reception
at once relieved and encouraged her to open her whole
heart. The interview was blessed of God to her conversion. And from that day, her course was remarkably direct and upward. She was, in a word, an
earnest, self-denying follower of Christ.

At the age of eighteen, by the aid of friends, she
was made a free woman ; and very soon afterwards
married ; but her husband and children did not live
long.

She lived in a part of the city where there were

many very poor families, and many of both colored
and white children who had none to care for their
bodies or souls. Some of these she took to her own
home and taught them to take care of themselves ;
and for others she found places, where they would
be provided for. In this way, during her life, she
secured homes for *forty-eight* of these neglected and
suffering ones ;—thus anticipating one of the benevolent movements of our time.

But her concern for the spiritual welfare of those
around⁻ her was especially manifest, and in most appropriate ways. She invited the children to come
into her house every Sabbath day, for religious instruction. Feeling her own incompetency to instruct
them fully, especially as she was herself unable to
read, she obtained the assistance of other Christian
people in this work. The well-known Isabella Graham
thus aided Katy by occasionally inviting her little
flock to come to her own house.

Thus Katy's labor of love went on for some time,
unobserved for the most part, even by Christian people, but not unnoticed by God. He smiled upon her,
and as He often does in the case of humble efforts
like hers, made her little school on the Sabbath the
beginning of a great and good work in that city. It
was about this time that the house of worship on
Murray street, in which Dr. Mason preached, was
built. This good man of God had not forgotten
Katy, the trembling inquirer. Having heard of her
Sabbath assembly of children, he went one day to see

what she was doing. As he entered her lowly dwelling, and looked around upon the group of interested, happy-looking faces, he said, with his wonted kindness: " What are you about here, Katy? Keeping school on the Sabbath? We must not leave you to do all this." He immediately conferred with the officers of his church, telling them what he had seen, and advising that others should join Katy in this good work. Soon the lecture-room was opened for the reception and instruction of Katy's charge. This was the beginning of the Sabbath-school in the Murray Street Church; and KATY FERGUSON, the colored woman, who had been a slave, is believed to have thus gathered THE FIRST SABBATH SCHOOL IN THE CITY OF NEW YORK.

But Katy's benevolent heart was not satisfied with this effort for the good of children. She established and maintained, during the last forty years of her life, a weekly prayer-meeting at her house, and during the last five years of her life, when she could not attend the public services of divine worship, she made her own house a Bethel on Sabbath afternoons, by gathering the neglected children of the neighborhood, with such others as did not attend at any place of public worship, and obtaining some suitable person to lead in the services of prayer and praise.

The cause of foreign missions was also dear to Katy. On one occasion, a young man who was about to sail for Africa as a missionary, was invited to attend a meeting at her house. Three years afterwards, on speaking of this man and his associate missionaries, she said : " For these three years I have never missed a day but I have prayed for those dear missionaries."

The question may occur to some persons, where did this poor woman procure the means of doing so much good—clothing children and assisting missionaries? Uneducated as she was, she possessed extraordinary taste and judgment. Of a truly refined nature, she appreciated the beautiful, wherever found. Hence a wedding, or other festival, in some of the best circles of New York, could scarcely be considered complete unless Katy had superintended the nicer provisions of the table. She was also uncommonly skilful in the cleaning of laces and other fine articles of ladies' dresses. This constant demand for her services must, however, be likewise traced, in part, to the great esteem in which she was held, and to the desire to furnish her the means of continuing her useful Christian labors.

She was a cheerful believer ; occupied less in complaining of her own deficiencies and her troubles, or boasting of her attainments, than in commending her Redeemer to others, and in trying to imitate His active benevolence.

Thus was this beloved disciple ripening for heaven. And when death, in that fearful disease, the cholera, came for her, she was ready, and calmly expressed her Christian confidence by saying : " Oh, what a good thing it is to have a hope in Jesus ! " Her last words were, " All is well."

POOR POMPEY.

An old African who had long served the Lord,
when on his death-bed, was visited by his friends, who
came around him lamenting that he was going to die,
saying : " Poor Pompey ! poor Pompey is dying." The
old saint said to them, with much earnestness : " Don't
call me poor Pompey. *I*, KING Pompey," referring to
Revelation i. verse 6.—*"And hath made us kings and
priests unto God and His Father."*

ANCASS.

" I WAS born in Africa, about the year 1789; the
country of the Iboes was my home. My father's
name was Durl, and mine, Ancass. My mother was
my father's only wife, and she was the daughter of a
great chieftain. Of four children I was the only son,
and therefore my father's pet. He always liked to
have me near him, and even when he went out to
work he would take me along with him. In the
midst of our ignorance we had a vague idea of the
existence of a Supreme Being, which we know that
every heathen can see from the works of creation.
We called him ' Thunderer,' and appealed to him for
aid in case of illness.

" A young man began to pay us frequent visits, under pretence of wishing to marry one of my sisters, but
in reality, doubtless, with a view to getting possession
of me, a growing, healthy boy, about twelve years old.

One day my father had gone out, leaving me with my sisters, and the young man made use of the opportunity to persuade me to accompany him to a market in the vicinity, which he described to me in glowing colors. We' walked all that day, and never reached the place; the night was spent with an acquaintance of my guide, and our journey continued all the next day. I was struck by the circumstance that persons who met us often asked the man what he was going to do with the boy he had with him, whether he was intending to sell him, etc. He invariably gave an assurance of the contrary, but I was soon to learn what his scheme really was.

" The end of the journey was reached at last, and proved to be a trading place on the coast. I lay down under a large tree, and gazed on the scene with delight.

" Suddenly a stranger appeared, and proposed that I should try a sail in his boat. I was frightened and refused : but found myself seized by the man's strong hand, and rapidly dragged away. Then I knew that I was being taken as a slave. The man who had brought me from home and sold me to the traders, looked on unmoved as I was hurried to the water's edge, and I could only implore him to take a last message to my dear father, letting him know what had become of me.

" There were several negroes already in the boat, bound with ropes, and others were added. When the boat put off for the ship I was so exhausted with

crying, that the gentle rocking motion lulled me into
a sound sleep, from which I awoke to find that we
were being lifted into the vessel. The white color of
the captain's face filled me with no less astonishment
than his black, shining feet without toes, as I regarded his polished boots, which I now saw for the first
time. The next morning I was horrified to see great
numbers of people brought up from the hold on deck,
to be fed with yams and rum. As for myself, I was
heartily glad to be spared this confinement. I was at
liberty to remain on deck with some other boys, slept
in the captain's cabin, and was soon very happy.

  " On reaching Kingston, in Jamaica, the slaves went
ashore, and I looked with intense longing at the
beautiful land, visible from the ship. I was kept on
board for several weeks, and the captain told me I
was destined to be his servant, and should not be
allowed to go ashore. On my declaring, however,
that I was resolved, at all hazards, to leave the vessel,
and would leap overboard if he should try to prevent
me, he changed his mind, and I was sent to a white
man, who took me, with eleven others, into the yard
adjoining his house. We were purchased for the
owner of the estate Krepp, and thither we were taken
without further delay. My companions were sent to
work in the fields ; I was retained as servant in the
overseer's family, and called Toby. After the lapse
of a year my master took me as servant into his own
house, making me the companion and play-fellow of
his children, and treating me with great kindness.

"About eight years afterwards my master left the island for England, and I was sent with the children to the seaport-town, Savana-la-Mar, where we were to attend the church and school. This was anything but agreeable to us, and I persisted in neglecting every opportunity of learning, which I might have enjoyed. As to the church, I invariably played outside during the services, and my master's children were generally with me. In three years' time the master returned, and took us all back to the estate, where he soon died. The eldest son became owner of the property, and he immediately appointed me his overseer at Krepp, and subsequently at Dumbasken, when the former estate was sold.

"In the year 1824 the owner of a neighboring estate (Paynstown) returned to Jamaica from a visit in England. This gentleman and his lady were true Christians. One evening, when passing his plantation on my way home, I met a female servant of the family, Christina by name, who was going to draw water from a neighboring spring. I entered into conversation with her, and she told me that on Sunday there would be prayer and singing at Paynstown, and that her master invited his people to attend. I asked if strangers were admitted, and was told that Mrs. Cook had frequently expressed her regret that no one from the vicinity would come to join them at prayers, and that strangers would be welcomed; not only on Sundays, but also in the morning and evening of the week-days.

"This conversation made a deep impression upon me, and the thought of the prayer-meeting at Paynstown was continually recurring day and night, until I at length resolved to go there on the following Sunday.

"Sunday came, and I started on my way to Paynstown. On reaching the house, a negro servant addressed me in a friendly voice; at the same moment Mrs. Cook appeared at the door, and I heard her say to the attendant, on his mentioning my name, 'Let him enter; I am glad that he comes!' Feeling very shy, I waited outside the hall till a bell gave the summons for prayers. Mr. Cook conducted the service, which was commenced with singing a hymn: then a portion of the Scriptures was read and prayer offered. I have no recollection of what was read, nor could I understand the prayer, as I knew nothing of our Saviour; yet I shall never forget this hour; it was a turning-point for the whole of my life. I had a feeling that I was in the presence of Almighty God, *my* Lord and God, and my inmost soul was deeply moved, while I trembled from head to foot. Unable to utter a word, I hurried away and remained alone in my hut.

"Some time afterwards Mrs. Cooper offered to teach me to read if I wished to learn, and I gladly accepted her offer, though exposing myself to no little ridicule on the part of my fellow-slaves, who thought it very foolish of me to attempt to learn to read 'the white men's book.' How thankful have I felt ever since that I was enabled to read the Bible for myself, and thus come into the enjoyment of a wonderful privilege !

" Saturday and Sunday were free days for the slaves ; Sunday was market-day in the neighboring town, and we negroes were in the habit of cultivating our own plots of ground on our return from the service at .Paynstown, or carrying their produce to the market. One Sunday I was so eagerly bent on making the most out of my garden, that I did not go to Paynstown, but was busy at work from earliest dawn. Suddenly the conviction seized my mind that I was not acting right in the sight of God, in thus digging and planting in hope of gain. Quite overcome with the thought, I threw away my hoe, and kneeling in the hole which I had just dug, I cried aloud to our Saviour, imploring Him to help me in my darkness, and show me what I ought to do. The comforting light was vouchsafed to me at once. While recognizing my sinful conduct in striving for outward gain to the detriment of my soul, I was assured that all my need would be supplied from the bountiful hand of my heavenly Father, and that the right course for me was to seek first the kingdom of God and His righteousness. From that day I never touched a hoe on Sunday, and I have been so blessed in regard to externals that I have never suffered any want.

" Some time afterwards I made a proposal of marriage to a young woman, whom I had known as one of the most regular attendants at the services in Mr.

Cooper's house, and she accepted it. My master and
mistress were at first greatly opposed to this step, but
were led eventually to withdraw their prohibition,
and we were married on the 8th of June, 1826.

"A few months afterwards I became a member of
the Moravian Church, one of twelve, who at that
time constituted the whole congregation. Many
others, however, joined the church at Carmel, and
the number of those who desired to cast in their lot
with us as children of God, increased most surprisingly from week to week.

"The office of native helper, to which I was soon
afterwards appointed, gave me many opportunities of
telling others what the Lord had done for me, and
directing them to the same Saviour.

"I had a great desire to purchase my freedom. I
went to my master, who tried to persuade me to
wait, seeing that I should be legally emancipated in
three years' time. My longing for freedom was, however, so strong that I remained unmoved. I paid
down all my savings, and was soon afterwards able to
complete the required sum, and my certificate of freedom was signed. O how full my heart was! how
overflowing with thanks and praise to God! This
day has always been to me a day of special rejoicing
and thanksgiving. It was the 1st of June, 1837.

"Subsequently I was asked by several gentlemen
to undertake the management of their estates, but I
declined, not wishing to fetter myself in such a manner as would be prejudicial to my work in the Lord's,

cause. I was greatly rejoiced when Brother Zorn proposed to me to devote my time entirely to the duties of a native helper, receiving £12 a year to provide subsistence for myself and family. I purchased a small cottage and piece of ground, and here I have lived ever since with my dear wife and the only daughter whom the Lord has been pleased to give us."

Ancass died July, 1864.—*English Tract.*

A STORM AT SEA.

SOME few years since, a minister was preaching at Plymouth, when a request was sent to the pulpit to this effect : " The thanksgiving of this congregation is desired to Almighty God, by the captain, passengers, and crew of a West Indiaman, for their merciful deliverance during the late tempest."

The following day the minister went on board, and entered into conversation with the passengers, when a lady thus addressed him : " O, sir, what an invaluable blessing is personal religion ! Never did I see it so exemplified as in my poor Ellen during the storm. When we expected every wave to entomb us all, my mind was in a horrible state—I was afraid to die. Ellen would come to me and say, with all possible composure : ' Never mind, missie ; look to Jesus Christ. He made—he rule the sea.' And

when we neared the shore, and were at a loss to know
where we were, fearing every minute to strike on the
rocks, Ellen said, with the same composure as before,
' Don't fear, missie; look to Jesus Christ—He the
Rock; *no shipwreck on that Rock;* He save to the
uttermost. Don't fear, missie; look to Jesus
Christ ! ' "

The minister wished to see this poor, though rich
African. She was called, and, in the presence of the
sailors, the following conversation took place :

Minister. " Well, Ellen, I am glad to find you
know something of Jesus Christ."

Ellen. " Jesus Christ, massá! Oh, He be very
good to my soul ! Oh ! He be very dear to me."

Minister. " How long since you first knew the
Saviour ? "

Ellen. " Why, some time ago me hear Massa Kitchin preach about the blessed Jesus. He say to us
colored people—the Lord Jesus come down from the
good world; He pity us poor sinners; we die, or He
die; *He die, but we no die.* He suffer on the cross—
He spill precious blood for us poor sinners. Me feel
me sinner; me cry; me pray to Jesus, and He save
me by His precious blood."

Minister. " And when did you see Mr. Kitchin
last ? "

Ellen. " Sir, the fever take him; he lie bed; he
call us his children. He say, ' Come round the bed,
my children.' He then say, ' My children, I go to
God; meet me before God;' and then he fall asleep."

Minister. " Oh, then, Mr. Kitchin is dead, is he ?"

Ellen. " Dead, sir ? oh, no ! Mr. Kitchin no die; he fall asleep in Jesus. He has gone to heaven."

" LITTLE WA."

THERE is a boy of tender years now in England, whose story beautifully illustrates the loving care of God for an afflicted heathen child. He is the son of an African chief, and two or three years since you might have seen him playing about his father's and mother's yard—as happy as the day was long—no kid frisked so merrily, no kitten was fuller of fun. But " little Wa" was deaf and dumb, and soon his mother, "Ti Bla," was to die, and then his father, " Ta Qwia," was to be laid by her side under the palm-tree. God foreknew this, and see how graciously He provided for this helpless orphan.

Little Wa was very fond of wandering from home ; and wherever he went, whether to the huts of the natives or the houses of the colonists, he was a great favorite, and everybody treated him kindly. He liked to sport about with those of his own age, and would amuse the tribes by the hour. Often he came to the mission station, and the missionary got quite attached to him, and encouraged him to stay, and gave him a white shirt—his first civilized suit. This delighted him, and kept him hovering around for a week together; then off he trotted to the town.

By-and-by he reappeared with his shirt dirty, and the missionary exchanged it for a clean one. "He seemed so pleased to be with us, and was such a good boy," says the missionary, "that pitying his sad case, I thought I would try and get him into my family." He asked his father, who was still an idolater, if he would let him keep him. His father said, "Yes, he might keep him if he could." He meant that "Wa" was such a gad-about that no one could keep him. However, the missionary determined to try it. He had some new clothes made for him, bound with scarlet; he set him a stool to have his meals, and he had his own plate and fork, and a snug corner to sleep in at night, and a warm blanket to wrap himself in.

Now, do you suppose that "Wa" stayed with the missionary, or that he ran away? He stayed, and he grew fonder and fonder of the missionary and the missionary of him. Whenever he ate his meals, before tasting anything, he would bend his head and shut his eyes, and be still, as if he was saying grace. So also, night and morning, he would always drop on his knees, and for a time remain in the attitude of prayer. Occasionally he would go into the school-room, and sitting beside the girls, take a book, and make believe that he was studying his lessons. The missionary would frequently have him in his room, and kneel down with him, and pray God to teach him by His Holy Spirit, and deliver him from all evil. God did indeed watch over him, and preserve him from danger, to which he was exposed. No lion was permitted to terrify him; and no scorpion or serpent was allowed to bite his bare feet. The angels had charge of him.

When, on account of his bad health, the missionary had to leave Africa for a season, he much desired to bring "little Wa" to England with him. He had a talk with his father (his mother was now dead) about it. He told him what Christian people had done in England for the deaf and dumb, what attention was paid to them, and how they were taught to write and read. He looked very serious, and shook his head. "I can't let him go;" he said, "I let his brother, 'Wia,' go to New York, and he is buried there. I can't let 'Wa' go." But when he assured him that England had a milder climate than New York, and that he would be a parent to him, and that it was only the child's welfare he sought, "Well," he said, "I will consider it." Shortly after he called and said, "Take him; do with him what you choose. He is yours." So the missionary began at once to get him ready for sea. He was fitted with red and yellow flannel smocks and trousers; and when he saw the preparations, and knew that he was going, he jumped for joy.

At length the steamer hove in sight. The captain agreed to charge a shilling a day for the "coal scuttle," as he called him. So he was brought off with them in a boat through the surf, and he bade adieu to the scenes of his infancy, in better spirits than the missionary did; but soon the rocking of the ship upset him. He lay down sick on the deck. When he recovered, he became a great favorite with the passengers and crew. He had a wonderful power of mimicry, and he amused many with his imitations. Now he would act as he saw the monkeys or the chimpanzee act; now he would mock the way in which the gentlemen walked when the vessel rolled; now he would pretend to be preaching; now he would dance as his country people do; and now, when a lady would be moving about alone, he would run up to her and offer her his arm. The officers would feed him with good things, and let him sleep in their state-rooms, though he had a comfortable box of his own.

When the missionary arrived at Liverpool, "little Wa" was an object of curiosity to all. His dark skin and his flaming-colored dress made him ridiculously conspicuous. The children in the streets followed him, and gathered round the shop-doors pointing at him jeeringly; but whenever they were rude the missionary said to them, "He is deaf and dumb," and then they would say, "Poor boy! poor little fellow!" You may be sure he was in ecstasies at the sights, such as he had never even dreamt of. Especially he noticed the horses, and tried to trot as they trot; and the sliders on the ice, and when one tumbled down he was convulsed with laughter. I have had him at my table, and he behaved himself like a gentleman, only he would open the whole plate of sandwiches to see which had least mustard on it; and when I presented him with a pear, he wanted to put it into his mouth whole.

It was decided that he should go into the Bath Deaf and Dumb Institution. The money, a large sum, was speedily raised by the ladies of Brighton. Far and wide contributions flowed in. "Little Wa" was loaded with presents beside; indeed, ladies began to be so kind to him that it was high time he was out of the way of being spoiled. News of his father's death reached England by the next mail; so now the missionary felt that "little Wa" was wholly his, and he took him to Bath without any further doubt as to its being God's will for him.

Before "little Wa" left London, he stole into the missionary's wife's sick chamber, and seeing that several persons were with her, he sat down quietly until they withdrew, then he quickly touched her; and then raising his eyes, he clasped his hands, and by other signs gave her to understand that he wished her to pray with him. She did so. On getting up, he looked into her face so bright and satisfied, and shook her hand to thank her. As he bade her good-bye, he signified that after two days and two nights he would come back to her. When the missionary was leaving him at the Institution, and broke the in- telligence to him that he must stay there a long while, "little Wa" was downcast for a moment, but he did not cry; he nodded his head bravely, and stood watching him at the door till he turned the corner.

A recent letter informed us that at first he showed considerable self-will, but was daily improving. If we recollect how short a time he has been under control at all, we cannot but wonder that the wild African is as tractable as he is. When he saw the handwriting of the missionary the tears started, and he pressed the envelope to his lips.

Now, my dear young readers, does not this narrative *prove* that God thinks of children, and loves them, and cares for them? He is busy with the affairs of the universe, and yet He can turn from them to provide for a heathen mute. He dwells in the high and holy place, and yet He can stoop to be a friend to the fatherless African boy. Who is a God like unto Him? Oh, give your heart to Him, that *you*, too, may have His wing spread over you, and be able to confide in Him for whatever you want.

May "little Wa's" Almighty protector and all-loving provider be yours!— *The Family Treasury.*

THE AFRICAN SERVANT.

DURING a residence of some years' continuance in the neighborhood of the sea, an officer in the navy called upon me and stated that he had just taken a lodging in the parish for his wife and children, and that he had an African whom he had kept three years in his service.

"Does he know anything," I asked, "of the principles of the Christian religion?"

"Oh, yes, I am sure he does," answered the captain; "for he talks a great deal about it in the kitchen, and often gets laughed at for his pains; but he takes it all very patiently."

"Does he behave well as your servant?"

"Yes, that he does: he is as honest and civil a fellow as ever came aboard a ship or lived in a house."

"Was he always so well-behaved?"

"No," said the officer; "when I first had him he was often very unruly and deceitful; but for the last two years he has been quite like another creature."

"Well, sir, I shall be very glad to see him, and think it probable I shall wish to go through a course of instruction and examination. Can he read?"

"Yes," replied his master; "he has been taking great pains to learn to read for some time past, and can make out a chapter in the Bible pretty well, as my maid-servant informs me. He speaks English better than many of his countrymen, but you will find it a little broken. When will it be convenient that I should send him over to you?" .

"To-morrow afternoon, sir, if you please."

"He shall come to you about four o'clock, and you shall see what you can make of him."

With this promise he took his leave. I felt glad to see him the next day, and asked:

" Where were you born ? "

" In Africa. I was very little boy when I was made slave by the white men."

" How was that ? "

" I left father and mother one day at home to go to get shells by the sea-shore ; and, as I was stooping down to gather them up, some white sailors came out of a boat and took me away. I never see father nor mother again."

" And what became of you then ? "

" I was put into ship and brought to Jamaica, and sold to a massa, who keep me in his house to serve him some years ; when about three years ago, Captain W——; my massa that spoke to you, bought me to be his servant on board his ship. And he be good massa ; and I live with him ever since."

" And what thoughts had you about your soul all that time before you went to America ? " I asked him.

" I no care for my soul at all before then. No man teach me a word about my soul."

" Well, now tell me further about what happened to you in America. How came you there ? "

" My massa take me there in a ship, and he stop there one month ; and then I hear the good minister."

" And what did that minister say ? "

" He said I was a great sinner."

" Did he speak to you in particular ? "

" Yes, I think so ; for there was a great many to hear him, but he tell them all about me."

" What did he say ? "

" He say all about the things that were in my heart."

" Who taught you to read ? "

" God teach me to read."

" What do you mean by saying so ? "

" God gave me desire to read, and that make reading easy. Massa give me Bible, and one sailor show me the letter ; and so I learn to read by myself with God's good help."

" And what do you read in the Bible? "

"Oh, I read all about Jesus Christ, and How He loved sinners ; and wicked men killed him, and He died and came again from the grave, and all this for poor negro. And it sometime make me cry to think that Christ love me so."

Not many days after the first interview with my African disciple, I went from home on horseback, with the design of visiting and conversing with him again at his master's house, which was situated in a part of the parish near four miles distant from my own. The road which I took lay over a lofty down or hill, which commands a prospect of scenery seldom equalled for beauty and magnificence. It gave birth to silent, but instructive contemplation.

As I pursued the meditations which this magnificent and varied scenery excited in my mind, I approached the edge of a tremendous perpendicular cliff with which the hill terminates; I dismounted from my horse and tied him.

I cast my eye downwards a little to the left, towards a small cove, the shore of which consists of fine hard sand. It is surrounded by fragments of rock, chalk cliffs, and steep banks of broken earth. Shut out from human intercourse and dwellings, it seems formed for retirement and contemplation. On one of these rocks I unexpectedly observed a man sitting with a book, which he was reading. The place was near two hundred yards perpendicularly below me : but I soon discovered by his dress, and by the color of his features, contrasted with the white rocks beside him, that it was no other than my African disciple, with, as I doubted not, a Bible in his hand. I rejoiced at this unlooked-for opportunity of meeting him in so solitary and interesting a situation. I descended a steep bank, winding by a kind of rude staircase, formed by fishermen and shepherds' boys, in the side of the cliff down to the shore.

He was intent on his book, and did not perceive me till I approached very near to him.

" William, is that you ? "

" Ah, massa, I very glad to see you. How came massa into this place ? I thought nobody here but only God and me."

" I was coming to your master's house to see you, and rode round by this way for the sake of the prospect. I often come here in fine weather to look at the sea and the shipping. Is that your Bible ? "

" Yes, sir, this is my dear, good Bible."

"I am glad," said I, "to see you so well employed; it is a good sign, William."

"Yes, massa, a sign that God is good to me; but I never good to God."

"How so?"

"I never thank Him enough; I never pray to Him enough; I never remember enough who give me all these good things. Massa, I afraid my heart very bad. I wish I was like you."

"Like me, William? Why, you are like me, a poor helpless sinner."

"Tell me, William, is not that very sin which you speak of, a burden to you? You do not love it: you would be glad to obtain strength against it, and to be freed from it, would you not?"

"Oh, yes; I give all this world, if I had it, to be without sin."

"Come then, and welcome, to Jesus Christ, my brother; His blood cleanseth from all sin. He gave himself as a ransom for sinners. He hath borne our griefs, and carried our sorrows. He was wounded for our transgressions, He was bruised for our iniquities; the chastisement of our peace was upon Him; and with His stripes we are healed. The Lord hath laid on Him the iniquity of us all. Come, freely come to Jesus, the Saviour of sinners."

"Yes, massa," said the poor fellow, weeping, "I will come, but I come very slow; very slow, massa; I want to run; I want to fly. Jesus is very good to poor me to send you to tell me all this."

I was much pleased with the affectionate manner in which he spoke of his parents, from whom he had been stolen in his childhood; and his wishes that God might direct them by some means to the knowledge of the Saviour.

"Who knows," I said, "but some of these ships may be carrying a missionary to the country where they live, to declare the good news of salvation to your countrymen, and to your own dear parents in particular, if they are yet alive."

"Oh, my dear father and mother; my dear, gracious Saviour," exclaimed he, leaping from the ground, as he spoke, "if Thou would but save their souls, and tell them what Thou hast done for sinners; but—"

He stopped and seemed much affected.

"My friend," said I, "I will now pray with you for your own soul, and those of your parents also."

"Do, massa, that is very good and kind; do pray for poor negro souls here and everywhere."

This was a new and solemn "house of prayer." The sea-sand was our floor, the heavens were our roof. The cliffs, the rocks, the hills, and the waves, formed the walls of our chamber. It was not indeed a "place where prayer was wont to be made," but for this once it became a hallowed spot; it will by me ever be remembered as such. The presence of God was there. I prayed. The African wept. His heart was full. I felt with him, and could not but weep likewise.

The last day will show whether our tears were not the tears of sincerity and Christian love.

I had, for a considerable time, been accustomed to meet some serious persons once a week, in a cottage at no great distance from the house where he lived, for the purpose of religious conversation, instruction, and prayer. Having found these occasions remarkably useful and interesting to myself and others, I thought it would be very desirable to take the African there, in order that there might be many witnesses to the simplicity and sincerity of real Christianity, as exhibited in the character of this promising young convert. I hoped it might prove an eminent means of grace to excite and quicken the spirit of prayer and praise among some over whose spiritual progress I was anxiously watching.

It was known that the African was to visit the little society this evening, and satisfaction beamed in every countenance as I took him by the hand and introduced him among them, saying, " I have brought a brother from Africa to see you, my friends. Bid him welcome in the name of the Lord."

" Sir," said a humble and pious laborer, whose heart and tongue always overflowed with Christian kindness, " we are at all times glad to see our dear minister, but especially so to-day, in such company as you have brought with you. We have heard how gracious the Lord has been to him. Give me your hand, good friend," turning to the African ; " God be with you here and everywhere ; and blessed be His holy name for calling wicked sinners, as I hope He has done you and me, to love and serve Him for His mercy's sake."

Each one greeted him as he came into the house, and some addressed him in very kind and impressive language.

" Massa," said he, " I not know what to say to all these good friends; 1 think this looks like little heaven upon earth."

He then, with tears in his eyes, which, almost before he spoke, brought responsive drops into those of all present, said :

" Good friends and brethren in Christ Jesus, God bless you all, and bring you to heaven at last."

After some time passed in more general conversation on the subject of the African's history, I said, " Let us now praise God for the rich and unspeakable gift of His grace, and sing the hymn of ' redeeming love,'

> " ' Now begin the heavenly theme,
> Sing aloud in Jesus' name,' " etc.

which was accordingly done. Whatever might be the merit of the natural voices, it was plain there was melody in all their hearts.

The African was not much used to our way of singing, yet joined with great earnestness and affection, which showed how truly he felt what was uttered. When the fifth verse was ended—

> " Nothing brought Him from above,
> Nothing but redeeming love "—

he repeated the words, almost unconscious where he was.

"No, nothing, nothing but redeeming love bring Him down to poor William; nothing but redeeming love."

The following verses were added, and sung by way of conclusion:

> See, a stranger comes to view;
> Though he's black, he's comely too:
> Come to join the choirs above,
> Singing of redeeming love.
>
> Welcome, brother, welcome here,
> Banish doubt, and banish fear;
> You, who Christ's salvation prove,
> Praise and bless redeeming love.
>
> —*Abridged from Legh Richmond.*

THE BLIND SLAVE IN THE MINES.

WITH a companion I had descended a thousand feet perpendicularly, beneath the earth's surface, into one of the coal mines of East Virginia, called the Mid-Lothian pit. As we were wandering through its dark passages—numerous and extensive enough to form a subterranean city—the sound of music at a little distance caught our ears. It ceased upon our approach; but we perceived that it was sacred music, and we heard the concluding sentiment of the hymn, "I shall be in heaven in the morning."

On advancing with our lamps we found the passage closed by a door, in order to give a different direction to the currents of air for the purpose of ventilation ; yet this door must be opened occasionally to let the rail-cars pass, loaded with coal. And to accomplish this we found sitting by that door an aged blind slave, whose eyes had been entirely destroyed by a blast of gunpowder many years before, in that mine. There he sat, on a seat cut in the coal, from sunrise to sunset, day after day ; his sole business being to open and shut the door when he heard the rail-cars approaching. We requested him to sing again the hymn whose last line we had heard. It was, indeed, lame in expression, and in poetic measure very defective, being in fact one of those productions which we found the pious slaves were in the habit of singing, in part at least, impromptu. But each stanza closed with the sentiment, "I shall be in heaven in the morning."

It was sung with a clear and pleasant voice, and I could see the shrivelled, sightless eyeballs of the old man rolling in their sockets, as if his soul felt the inspiring sentiments ; and really the exhibition was one of the most affecting that I have ever witnessed. There he stood, an old man, whose earthly hopes, even at the best, must be very faint—and he was a slave— and he was blind—what could he hope for on earth ? He was buried, too, a thousand feet beneath the solid rocks. In the expressive language of Jonah, he had "gone down to the bottom of the mountains ; the earth with her bars was about him for ever." There, from month to month, he sat in total darkness.

I would add, that on inquiry of the pious slaves engaged in these mines, I found that the blind old man had a fair reputation for piety, and that it was not till the loss of his eyes that he was led to the Saviour. It may be that the destruction of his natural vision was the necessary means of opening the eye of faith within his soul. And though we should shudder at the thought of exchanging conditions with him on earth, yet who can say but his peculiar and deep tribulation here may prepare his soul for a distinction in glory which we might covet. Oh, how much better to endure even his deep degradation and privations, sustained by his hopes, than to partake of their fortune who live in luxury and pleasure, or riot in wealth!

The scene which I have now described affords a most animating lesson of encouragement to the tried and the afflicted, and of reproof to the complaining and discontented.

Suppose health does fail us, and poverty oppress us, and our friends forsake us, and our best laid plans prove abortive, so that a dark cloud settles upon our worldly prospects—who of us is reduced so low as to be willing to change places with this poor slave? And yet he is able to keep his spirits buoyant by the single hope of future glory. He thinks of a morning that is to come, when even his deep and dreadful darkness shall pass away; and the thought has a magic power to sustain him. If we are Christians, shall not that same hope chase away our despondency, and nerve us to bear cheerfully those trials which are far inferior to his?

THE AFRICAN SERVANT'S PRAYER.

I WAS a helpless negro boy,
  And wandered on the shore;
Men took me from my parents' arms,
  I never saw them more.

But yet my lot, which seemed so hard,
  Quite otherwise did prove;
For I was carried far from home,
  To learn a Saviour's love.

Poor and despiséd though I was,
  Yet Thou, O God, wast nigh;
And when Thy mercy first I saw,
  Sure none so glad as I.

And if Thy Son hath made me free,
  Then am I free indeed;
My soul is rescued from its chains;
  For this did Jesus bleed.

Oh, send Thy word to that far land
  Where none but negroes live;
Teach them the way, the truth, the life;
  Thy grace, Thy blessing give.

Oh, that my father, mother, dear,
    Might there Thy mercy see :
Tell them what Christ has done for them,
    What Christ has done for me.

Whose God is like the Christian's God ?
    Who can with Him compare ?
He has compassion on my soul,
    And hears a negro's prayer.

ANECDOTE.

A worthy old colored woman in the city of New
York was one day walking along the street on some
errand to a neighboring store, with her tobacco-pipe
in her mouth, quietly smoking. A sailor, rendered
mischievous by liquor, came down the street, and when
opposite Phillis, crowded her aside, and with a wave
of his hand knocked her pipe out of her mouth. He
then halted to hear her fret at his trick, and to enjoy
a laugh at her. But what was his astonishment when
she meekly picked up the pieces of her broken pipe,
without the least resentment in her manner, and giving him a look of mingled sorrow, kindness, and pity,
said : "God forgive my son, as I do." It touched
a tender part of the young sailor's heart; he felt
ashamed and repented ; the tears started in his eyes.
He confessed his error, and thrusting both hands into
his two full pockets of change, forced her to take the

handfuls of money, saying: " God bless you, kind
mother, I'll never do so again."

A LITTLE ACT OF KINDNESS.

ONE dull night I sat by my window watching the
people as they passed to and from the market. The
wind blew hard, and the rain was beginning to patter
against the window panes, and make large drops on
the pavement.

Soon I noticed two little colored girls hurrying past
with an empty basket, and I heard one of them say :
" Oh, be quick, for it is going to rain hard, and the
chips will all be wet."

" Yes, I'm coming in a minute," said the other,
who lingered behind — for what purpose, do you
think ?

Leaning against the lamp-post at the corner of the
street was a poor old woman, bent with age and in-
firmities.   In one hand was her market-basket, in the
other a bundle, and she was trying to open an umbrella.   The wind blew against her, the bundle slipped
from her poor old fingers, rolling into the gutter, and
the umbrella would not come open.

But the quick feet and fingers of this little girl
soon set things all right. First she hastened to res-
cue the bundle, and restore it to its owner; then
opened the umbrella and placed it securely in the

old woman's hands. She waited for no more—hastening on after her companion; but, amid the falling rain, I heard the old woman say, " God bless you, my child ! "

Ah ! it was a little deed, but done so cheerfully and quickly that I knew the child had a kind heart. Was the act not seen and noticed by our Father in heaven, and will He not bless the child who helps the aged and infirm?

Dear little ones, do not let *one chance* of helping another, or of doing good, pass by.

If your eyes are open, you will see these opportunities *every day*, and oh, how happy you may make your own heart, and the heart of some other, while your dear Father in heaven will smile upon your efforts.—*Angel of Peace.*

OLD SUSAN.

BY GERTRUDE L. VANDERBILT.

" BLESS de Lord, I'm pretty well, and granny's no wuss." I heard the voice below my window just as the dawn of a bright summer day was coloring the eastern horizon. Then another question was asked by the cook below, as she threw open the shutters, but I could only hear old Susan's reply: " No, I can't come in ; I'm up so airly to look for wood to bile the kittle. Granny'll be a-wantin' breakfast."

Soon after I saw the poor old woman bent almost double with the weight of fagots on her back, and her check apron filled with chips and corn-cobs from the wood-yard. I raised the sash, and called her :

"Aunt Susan, do come in ! Flora will get your breakfast, and you can take some home with you for granny," said I.

She lowered the bundle of fagots from her shoulders, and pushed back the long gingham sun-bonnet, as she looked up at my window.

" Bless yer heart, chile, but I couldn't—wouldn't ! " She shook her head very decidedly, and adjusted the red bandana turban which had been crushed down by the sun-bonnet. " Ye see, me and granny ain't had fambly prayers yit this morning. That's it ; obliged to yer jes' the same."

I suggested that our Heavenly Father would not reject prayers that were offered after breakfast. She looked up at me as I leaned from the window to catch the glory of the sunrise, and said, with rather a touch of sadness in her tone :

" No, chile, yer hadn't oughter think so. De Lord fust, an' everything else afterwards. Ef ye eat, or ef ye drink, do it all to de glory of God ; but it tain't ter IIis glory ef yer please yerself fust. I'll be round biemby ; then we 'splain the matter together." And reloading her tired shoulders, she tottered off under her burden.

This poor colored woman, bent down by her seventy years of sickness, and poverty, and hard work, and

constant care, had a conscience so tender that nothing
could have induced her to partake of the proffered
meal before she had offered up her morning prayer,
lest the act might seem like want of reverence and
respect.

This was not an occasional spasmodic outburst of
piety; she seemed always anxious to talk about God,
and, as she could not read herself, to hear others read
about Him. I never knew one who seemed to be in
such constant and close communion with God. In
my visits among the poor, I remember calling at her
door one day, and being obliged to wait some time
after knocking, although I heard her voice within. I
was surprised that she should keep me waiting, for
she had such a delicate sense of the duties of hospitality that she was particularly careful never to oblige
a visitor to remain standing at her door. I soon discovered that she was engaged in prayer; one greater
than any earthly guest was with her; it almost seemed
as if she pleaded before one who was visibly present.
She waited and wept, she urged, entreated, and
earnestly pleaded; then gradually her tone changed,
and her voice rose in prayer and loud hallelujahs,
and then she was silent. I knocked once more, and
hastily now she threw open the door; the traces of
tears were still on her cheeks, and in her poor, dim
eyes.

" Welcome, welcome ! " she exclaimed : " come in.
De Lord's bin wid me dis day. Praise and bless His
holy name. I'se had sich a blessed time."

Then she dusted the only spare seat her poor room afforded, and placed it so that as she seated herself upon her bed she should face me.

"Oh, chile!" she exclaimed; "de prayers dat's gone up from dis poor shanty for you and de Sunday-school! Dey's gone right up from dis poor, low, mean place, right up through dis old roof, straight up to de great white throne!" And she clasped her hands and looked up as if she saw the vision beyond. "God's holy angels has heard 'em, Jesus's listened to 'em, and God's treasured 'em up, and dey'll come down in blessin's when old Susan's dead and gone. When I gits rid of dis mis'able, sickly body, and rises up to where my prayer's gone before me, oh, how I'll sing wid de holy angels, praise de Lord, praise de Lord!"

She used to go off in these rhapsodies frequently; she had dull prosaic neighbors, who never got excited over praise or anything else, and they used to say that old Susan was crazy when she prayed. In alluding to this she once told me, smiling, that she was going to ask the Lord to make them crazy in prayer. She thought a little more earnestness on the subject would be an inprovement. Her faith was so strong that it seemed to have an element of sublimity in it; it was grand! The extreme poverty in which she lived, and her reliance upon others for every comfort in life, made her realize her dependence upon our Father in heaven more strongly than those who live in ease and luxury. She has often said to me, I am poor and sick, broken down with hard work, crooked and bent

with rheumatism, my wrists are so weak, and my
fingers so stiff, that I can hardly pick up chips ; boys
often laugh at me in the street, because when I bend
down I cannot always get up again; sometimes my
fire goes out, and I have nothing to eat until the
Lord sends some kind friend with food. But bless
the Lord I am going home. The Lord is my Father,
and in my Father's house there is plenty ; more than
enough. Oh, when I get home! Dear Lord, dear
Lord! When I shall reach my home, I shall forget
all the troubles I have had in this poor shanty.
Looking at her in her poor room, I have often
thought that if possible, heaven would seem more
glorious to her, coming out of distress and misery,
sickness and want, darkness and cold, into the full
blaze of heavenly light.

She was very grateful to those who paid her rent.
Of one lady in particular, she often spoke to me with
great affection. She said to me once, naming this-
lady : "She is to be paid back every cent." It was
spoken with so much earnestness that I involuntarily
looked around as if I expected to see some one standing
there with the money. She smiled, and told me she
had been reminding God of His promise to pay her
debts.

I once called on passing, to leave some dinner for
her, she met me at the door, and insisted on my coming in. "I know'd you was a comin'," she said, "for
I had nothin' t'eat, and I prayed de Lord ter send me
somethin'."

"Well," I replied, "He has heard your prayer, and has sent this to you."

She placed the dish on her stove to keep warm, and then she began to talk of prayer. "I does pray fur you," she said, "and fur Mr. and Mrs. L., and Miss C. I prays fur all de world, but the Lord lets us choose out those who's good to us, and pray fur them most of all. Mr. L. has been so good, so good to me, never gettin' tired of being good to me, oh, I do pray fur him!" She paused, and sat thinking a moment, and then added: "When Aunt Susan stops a prayin', she'll be cold and dead."

"Aunt Susan" was by no means a gloomy Christian, she had a sense of humor, and was often very quick-witted in reply.

During those terrible riots in New York, in which so many of her race fell victims to the mob, she fled to her white friends for protection. Some time after this, when she was speaking of her faith and her trust in the Lord, an Irish Roman Catholic taunted her with having failed to trust in the Lord at that time. Her reply was very characteristic. "Did you ever read in the Old Testament of a man named Lot?" she asked. "Well, Lot showed his faith by running away, and so did Aunt Susan!" In relating to me this story, she laughed very heartily, and concluded by saying: "Yer see as I understan's it, Lot showed his faith by leavin' his home and flyin' accordin' to the command of der Lord, and Aunt Susan did jes de same, fur I showed my faith by usin' de means de

Lord hed appinted, and not temptin' de Lord by stayin' behind. Jes so."

Old Susan's "family" consisted of her aged mother, at that time in her hundred and first year, her dog Prince, her cat Tom, her hen Toby ; a more aged and decrepit family were surely never before gathered under one roof. If I had been told that old Dinah's age was a hundred and twenty, from appearances I should have been inclined to believe it. Smoking was the sole recreation which years had left her. Susan would fill her pipe at intervals during the day, and after using it, Dinah would sit gazing vacantly around her until it was refilled and placed in her hand. The dog, proportionately to canine years, had reached an equally advanced age with his mistress, and his scabby back gave him the appearance of having been eaten by moth. The cat and the hen had reached a greater age than the time usually allotted to their species ; each would sit for hours perfectly motionless on the door-step, as if musing on the singing and exhorting they were constantly hearing within the house from their old mistress. Susan was very fond of animals, and seemed to have a curious power in taming and controlling them. I once told her, that had she lived earlier, she might have been taken up for a witch, with Tom and Toby as her familiar spirits.

Old Susan's faith led her to believe that she could see the hand of God in even the most trifling events of life, and that, as He was leading her, and teaching her through these means, she should be ever on the watch, so as not to lose the lessons His providence. set in her way. She came to me one day with the utmost gravity, to tell me of a lesson in resignation. This pet dog, through some inadvertence, had eaten a portion prepared for rats ; her tender heart was much troubled by the suffering so carelessly inflicted.   Just before extinguishing her light at night, she turned to Dinah and—to let her tell her own story, as she told it to me : " Sez I, granny, look yer last on poor Prince, fur you'll never see him alive no more. Then it kinder struck me that I wasn't resigned, so I kneels down, and sez I, ' O dear Lord, he's bin a faithful dog to me. He's watched over my things many a day when I was out a beggin' for daily bread ; he's bin very faithful, but I gin him up to de Lord.   If de Lord says his time's out, I gin him up.   I's re-signed.' Next mornin' I opens de winders, an' be-hold, dere's Prince, jis as well as ever !   Sez I, granny, de Lord has gin him back to me.   He was jis a tryin' my faith !   His will is the best fur us all, ye mus larn dat, granny, dat's the lesson from dis provi-dence."

Old Susan still lives, but her faculties seem gradu-ally failing, while life yet retains hold in her weak frame. She is helpless, poor, and old. While earthly matters seem fading out of her memory, her thoughts still cling to things above. In my last tract-distri-buting visit to her room, I found her holding an open Testament, with the leaf folded down at the fourteenth chapter of St. John's Gospel. She cannot read, but she sat pathetically looking at the text. As I entered, she exclaimed : " Oh, read it, read it, for me ! " It seemed as if her faith, so sorely tried by her long waiting, and her earthly sufferings, was for a moment wavering. As I slowly and distinctly read the words, " In my Father's house are many mansions," etc., the glimmering rays rekindled, her faith re-asserted itself. " Yes, yes ! " she exclaimed, " I knew it was so, I knew it was written somewhere there ; now I re-member it. I'll yet have a home in my Father's house." As I looked at the poor, worn-out frame ; the weak, helpless hands ; the wrinkled face, and the dim eyes, my faith could see through these the glori-ous spirit that should one day arise and take its up-ward flight towards the heavenly mansions.

POOR SARAH;

Or, Religion Exemplified in the Life and Death of a Pious Indian Woman.

The subject of the following narrative lived and died in a town in the eastern part of Connecticut. We are well acquainted with the writer, and we can assure our readers that the account here given is true.—*Editor of the Religious Intelligencer.*

IT was a comfortless morning in the month of March, 1814, when I first formed an acquaintance with the subject of the following sketch.

She called to solicit a few *crusts*, meekly saying she
" deserved nothing but the *crumbs*—they were enough
for her poor old body, just ready to crumble into
dust." I had heard of *Sarah*, a pious Indian
woman, and I was therefore prepared to receive her
with kindness. And remembering the words of my
Lord, who said, " Inasmuch as ye have done it unto
one of the *least* of these my brethren, ye have done it
unto me," I was ready to impart a portion of my *little*
unto her (for little, alas! was my store).

" And how," I asked her, " have you got along, this
long, cold winter, Sarah?" O misse," she replied,
" God better to Sarah than she fear. When winter
come on, Sarah was in great doubt. No husband, no
child here but one; she wicked, gone a great deal.
What if great snow come? What if fire go out?
Nabor great way off. What if sick all 'lone?
What if I die? Nobody know it.

" While I think so, in my heart, then I cry: while
I cryin', somethin' speak in my mind, and say, 'Trust
God, Sarah; He love His people, He never leave
them, He never forsake them; He never forsake Sarah,
He friend indeed. Go tell Jesus, Sarah; He love hear
prayer; He often hear Sarah pray.' So I wipe my
eyes; don't cry any more; go out in bushes, where
nobody see, fall down on my old knees and pray. God
give me great many words; pray a great while. God
make all my mind peace.

" When I get up, go in house, can't stop prayin' in
my mind. All my heart burn with love to God;

willin' live cold, go hungry, be sick, die all 'lone, if
God be there. He know best; Sarah don't know.
So I feel happy ; great many day go singin' hymn—

> 'Now I can trust the Lord for ever,
> He can clothe, and He can feed,
> He my rock, and He my Saviour,
> Jesus is a friend indeed.' "

"Well, Sarah, have you been comfortably supplied ? " "O yes," she replied, "I never out corn
meal once all winter." "But how do you cook it,
Sarah, so as to make it comfortable food ? " "O, I
make porridge, misse. Sometimes I get out, like to-
day, and I go get some crusts bread and some salt put
in it, then it is so nourishing to this poor old body ;
but when can't get none, then make it good I can,
and kneel down, pray God to bless it to me; and I
feel if God feed me, and be so happy here "—(laying
her hand on her heart).

Oh, what a lesson, thought I, for my repining heart !
"But do you have no meat or other necessaries,
Sarah ? " "Not often, misse ; sometimes I get so
hungry for it, I begin feel wicked ; then think how
Jesus hungry in the desert. But when Satan tempt
Him to sin, to get food, He would not. So I say, Sarah
won't sin to get victuals. I no steal, no eat stole
food, though be hungry ever so long.

"Then God gives me small look of His self, His *Son*,
and His glory; and I think in my heart, they all be

mine soon; then I no suffer hunger any more—my
Father have there many mansions." . "Sarah," said
I, "you seem to have some knowledge of the Scriptures; can you read?" "I can spell out a little; I
can't read like you white folks; O, if I could!" Here
she burst into tears. ‾

But after regaining her composure, she added,
"This, misse, what I want abov̊e all things, more than
victuals or drink. Oh, how often I beg God teach me
to read, and He do teach me some. When I take
Bible, kneel down and pray, he show me great many
words, and they be so sweet, I want to know a great
deal more. Oh, when I get home to heaven, then I
know all; no want to read any more."

In this strain of simple piety, she told me her first
interesting story. And when she departed, I felt a
stronger evidence of her being a true child of God,
than I have acquired of some professors by a long acquaintance. In one of the many visits she afterward
made me, she gave me, in substance, the following account of her conversion :—She lived, according to her
own account, until she became a wife and mother,
without hope and without God in the world, having
been brought up in extreme ignorance.

Her husband treating her with great severity, she
became dejected and sorrowful, and to use her own
simple language, "I go sorrow, sorrow, all day long.
When the night come, husband come home angry,
beat me so; then I think, Oh, if Sarah had friend!
Sarah no friend. I no want tell nabor I got trouble,

'Come,

stable, go suffer all His life, die on great cross, bury,
rise, and go up into heaven, to be always sinners'
friend. He say, too, if you got trouble, go to the
Lord Jesus. He best friend in sorrow, He cure all
your sorrow, He bring you out of trouble, He support
you, make you willin' suffer.

"So when I go home, think great deal what minister say; think this the friend I want—this the friend
I cry for so long. Poor ignorant Sarah never heard
so much about Jesus before. Then I try hard to tell
Jesus how I want such friend. But oh, my heart so
hard, can't feel, can't pray, can't love Jesus, though
he so good. This make me sorrow more and more.

"When Sunday come, want to go to Meetin' 'gain.
Husband say, 'You shan't go; I beat you if you go.'
So I wait till he go off huntin', then shut up children
safe, and run to Meetin'; sit down in door, hear minister tell how bad my heart is—no love to God, no
love to Jesus, no love to pray. So then I see why
can't have Jesus for friend, 'cause got so bad heart:
then go prayin' all way home, Jesus make my heart
better.

"When got home, find children safe, feel glad. husband no come: only feel sorry 'cause my wicked heart don't know how make it better. When I go sleep, then dream I can read good book : dream I read there, Sarah must be born 'gain. In mornin' keep thinkin' what that word mean. When husband go work, run over my good nabor, ask her if Bible say so.

"Then she read me, where that great man go see Jesus by night, 'cause 'fraid go in day-time. I think he just like Sarah. She must go in secret, to hear 'bout Jesus, else husband be angry, and beat her. Then feel 'couraged in mind, determined to have Jesus for friend. So asked nabor how get good heart. She tell me, ' Give your heart to Jesus, He will give Holy Spirit, make it better. Sarah don't know what she mean—never hear 'bout Holy Spirit.

"She say must go Meetin' next Sunday, she will tell minister 'bout me—he tell me what to do. So Sarah go hear how must be born 'gain ; minister say, 'You must go fall down 'fore God; tell Him you grieved 'cause you sin—tell him you want better heart—tell him for Christ Jesus' sake give Holy Spirit, make your heart new.' Then Sarah go home light, 'cause she know the way.

"When get home, husband beat me 'cause I go Meetin'—don't stay home work. I say, 'Sarah can't work any more on Sunday, 'cause sin 'gainst God. I rather work night, when moon shine.' So he drive me hoe corn that night, he so angry. I want to pray great deal, so go out hoe corn, pray all the time. When come in house, husband sleep. Then I kneel down and tell Jesus take my bad heart—can't bear bad heart; pray give me Holy Spirit, make my heart soft, make it all new.

"So great many days Sarah go beg for a new heart. Go Meetin' all Sundays; if husband beat me, never mind it; go hear good nabor read Bible every day. So, after great while, God make all my mind peace. I love Jesus; I love pray to Him; love tell Him all my sorrows. He take away my sorrow, make all my soul joy; only sorrow 'cause can't read Bible—learn how to be like Jesus; want to be like His dear people Bible tell of.

"So I make great many brooms; go get Bible for 'em. When come home, husband call me fool for it; say he burn it up. Then I go hide it; when he gone, get it, kiss it many times, 'cause it Jesus' good Word. Then I go ask nabor if she learn me read; she say, 'Yes.' Then I go many days learn letters, pray God all the while help me learn read His Holy Word.

"So, misse, I learn read hymn; learn to spell out many good words in Bible. So every day take Bible, tell my children that be God's words, tell 'em how Jesus die on cross for sinner: then make 'em all kneel down, I pray God give 'em new heart; pray for husband too, he so wicked. Oh, how I sorry for him; fear his soul go in burnin' flame."

"Sarah," said I, "how long did your husband live?" "Oh, he live great many year." "Did he repent and become a good man?" "No, misse, I 'fraid not; he sin more and more. When he got sick, I in great trouble for him; talk every day to him,

but he no hear Sarah. I say, 'How can you bear go
in burnin' fire, where worm never die, where fire never
go out?' At last he get angry, bid me hold my
tongue. So I don't say any more, only mourn over
him every day 'fore God.

"When he die, my heart say, 'Father, thy will be
done — Jesus do all things well. Sarah can't help him
now, he be in God's hands; all is well.' So then give
my heart all away to Jesus; tell Him I be all His;
serve Him all my life; beg Holy Spirit come fill all
my heart, make it all clean and white like Jesus.
Pray God help me learn more of His sweet words.

"And now, Sarah live poor Indian widow great
many long year; always find Jesus friend, husband,
brother, all. He make me willin' suffer; willin' live
great while in this bad world, if He see best. 'Bove
all, He give me great good hope of glory when I die.
So now I wait patient till my change comes."

While she was giving this narration, her countenance bore strong testimony to the diversified emotions
of her soul. I might greatly swell the list of particulars; but I design only to give the outlines of an example which would have done honor to the highest
sphere in life; and which, in my opinion, is not the
less excellent, or the less worthy of imitation, because
shrouded in the veil of poverty and sorrow. It was
evident she meditated much on what little she knew
of divine things; and what she knew of the Bible was
to her like honey and the honeycomb.

She was in the habit of bringing bags of sand into

the village, and selling it to buy food. Sometimes she
brought grapes and other kinds of fruit. But as she
walked by the way, she took little notice of anything
that passed (except children, whom she seldom passed
without an affectionate word of exhortation to be
good, say their prayers, learn to read the Bible, etc.,
accompanied with a bunch of grapes or an apple—thus
engaging the affection of many a little heart), but
seemed absorbed in meditation; and you might often
have observed her hands uplifted in the attitude of
prayer.

One day, after having observed her as she came, I
asked her how she could bring so heavy loads, old
as she was, and feeble. "Oh," said she, "when I got
great load, then I go pray God give me strength to
carry it. So I go on, thinkin' all the way how good
God is give His only Son die for poor sinner; think
how good Jesus be, suffer so much for such poor creature; how good Holy Spirit was, come into my bad
heart, make it all new : so these sweet thoughts make
my mind so full joy, I never think how heavy sand
be on my old back."

Here, said I to my heart, learn how to make the
heavy load of iron cares easy. One day she passed
with a bag of sand. On her return she called on me.
I inquired how much Mrs. —— gave her for the
sand. She was unwilling to tell, and I feared she was
unwilling lest I should withhold my accustomed
mite, on account of what she had already received ;
I therefore insisted she should let me see.

She at length consented, and I drew from the bag a
bone, not containing meat enough for half a meal.
" Is this all? Did that rich woman turn you off
so? How cruel, how hard-hearted ! " I exclaimed.
" Misse," she replied, " this made me 'fraid let you
see it; I 'fraid you would be angry : I hope she have
bigger heart next time, only she forget now that Jesus
promise to pay her all she give Sarah. Don't be angry, I pray God to give her a great deal bigger
heart."   •

The conviction, that she possessed, in an eminent
degree, the Spirit of Him who said, " Bless them that
curse you," and prayed for His murderers, rushed
upon my mind with energy, and I could compare myself in some measure to those who said, " Shall we
command fire to come down from heaven," etc. I
think I never felt deeper self-abhorrence and abase-
ment; I left her for a moment, and from the few
comforts I possessed, gave her a considerable portion.

She received them with the most visible marks of
gratitude—arose to depart, went to the door, and then
turned, looking me in the face with evident concern.
" Sarah," said I, " what would you have ? " (suppos-
ing she wanted something I had not thought of, and
she feared to ask). " Oh, my good misse ! " said she,
" nothing ; only 'fraid your big heart feel some proud
'cause you give more for nothing than Misse ———
for sand."

This faithfulness, added to her piety and gratitude,
completed the swell of feeling already rising in my

soul; and bursting into tears, I said, "O Sarah! when you pray that Mrs. —— may have a bigger heart, don't forget to pray that I may have an humbler one." " I will, misse, I will," she exclaimed with joy, and hastened on her way.

Another excellence in her character, was, that she loved the habitation of God's house, and often appeared there, when, from bad weather or other causes, many a seat of affluence was empty. She was always early; ever clean and whole in her apparel, though sometimes almost as much diversified with patches as the shepherd's coat.

She was very old and quite feeble, yet she generally stood during public service, with eyes riveted on the preacher. I have sometimes overtaken her on the steps, after service, and tapping her on her shoulder, would say, "Have you had a good day, Sarah?" "All good; sweeter than honey," she would reply.

In the spring of 1818, it was observed by her friends that she did not appear at Meeting as usual, and one of her particular female benefactors asked her the reason; when she, with streaming eyes, told her that her clothes had become so old and ragged that she could not come with comfort or decency; but said she had been praying God to provide for her in this respect, a great while, and telling Jesus how much she wanted to go to His house of prayer, and expressed a strong desire to be resigned and submissive to His will.

This was soon communicated to a few friends, who promptly obeyed the call of Providence, and soon furnished this suffering member of Christ with a very decent suit of clothes.   This present was almost over-powering to her grateful heart. She received them as from the hand of her Heavenly Father and kind Re-deemer, in answer to her special prayer.

But this did not in the least diminish her gratitude to her benefactors ; but she said she would go on, tell Jesus how good His dear people were to this poor old creature, and pray her good Father to give them great reward.   Two of the garments given her, she received with every mark of joy.   On being asked why she set so high a value on these, she replied, " Oh, these just what I pray for so long, so as to lay out my poor old body, clean and decent, like God's dear white people, when I die."

These she requested a friend to keep for her, fear-ing to carry them home, lest they should be taken from her.   She was, however, persuaded to wear one of them to Meeting, upon condition that if she injured that, another should be provided ; the other was pre-served by her friend, and made use of at her death.

Thus was this humble band of female friends hon-ored, by anointing, as it were, the body, beforehand, to the burial.   And I doubt not that her prayer was heard, and will be answered in their abundant re-ward.   The last visit I had from her was in the sum-mer of 1818.   She had attended a funeral, and on re-turning, she called at my cottage.   She complained of great weariness, and pain in her limbs, and showed me her feet, which were much swollen.

I inquired the cause. " Oh," said she, with a serene smile, " death comes creeping on ; I think in grave-yard to-day, Sarah must lie here soon." " Well, are you willing to die ? do you feel ready ? " " Oh, I hope, misse, if my bad heart tell true, I willin' and ready to do just as Jesus bid me. If He say, ' You must die,' I glad to go be with Him; if He say, ' Live, and suffer great deal more,' then I willin' do that; I think Jesus know best.

" Sometime I get such look of heaven, I long to go see Jesus; see happy angel; see holy saint; throw away my bad heart; lay down my old body ; and go where I no sin. Then I tell Jesus ; He say, ' Sarah, I prepare a place for you, then I come to take you to myself.' Then I be quite like child, don't want to go till He call me."

Much more she said upon this interesting subject, which indicated a soul ripe for heavenly glories. When we parted, I thought it very doubtful whether we should ever meet again below. In the course of three weeks I heard Sarah was dead.

THE GENEROUS NEGRO.

JOSEPH RACHEL resided in the island of Barbadoes. He was a trader, and dealt chiefly in the retail way. In his business, he conducted himself so fairly and

complaisantly, that in a town filled with little ped-
dling shops, his doors were thronged with customers.
Almost all dealt with him, and ever found him remarkably honest and obliging.

If any one knew not where to obtain an article,
Joseph would endeavor to procure it, without making
any advantage for himself. In short, his character was
so fair, and his manners so generous, that the best
people showed him a regard which they often deny
to men of their own color, because they are not
blessed with the like goodness of heart.

In 1756, a fire happened, which burned down a
great part of the town, and ruined many of the inhabitants. Joseph lived in a quarter that escaped
the destruction, and expressed his thankfulness by
softening the distresses of his ·neighbors. Among
those who had lost their property by this heavy misfortune, was a man to whose family Joseph, in the
early part of his life, owed some obligations.

This man, by too great hospitality, an excess very
common in the West Indies, had involved himself in
difficulties, before the fire happened; and his estate
lying in houses, that event entirely ruined him.
Amid the cries of misery and want, which excited
Joseph's compassion, this man's unfortunate situation
claimed particular notice. The generous and open
temper of the sufferer, the obligations that Joseph
owed to his family, were special and powerful motives for acting toward him the part of a friend.

Joseph had his bond for sixty pounds sterling.

" Unfortunate man," said he, "this debt shall never come against you. I sincerely wish you could settle all your other affairs as easily. But how am I sure that I shall keep in this mind? May not the love of gain, especially when, by length of time, your misfortune shall become familiar to me, return with too strong a current, and bear down my fellow-feeling before it? But for this I have a remedy. Never shall you apply for the assistance of any friend against my avarice."

He arose, and ordered a large account that the man had with him, to be drawn out; and in a whim that might have called up a smile, on the face of Charity, he filled his pipe, sat down again, twisted the bond and lighted his pipe with it. While the account was drawing out, he continued smoking, in a state of mind that a monarch might envy. When it was finished, he went in search of his friend, with the discharged account and the mutilated bond in his hand.

On meeting him, he presented the papers to him with this address: "Sir, I am sensibly affected with your misfortunes: the obligations I have received from your family give me a relation to every branch of it. I know that your inability to pay what you owe gives you more uneasiness than the loss of your own substance.

" That you may not be anxious on my account in particular, accept of this discharge, and the remains of your bond. I am overpaid in the satisfaction

that I feel from having done my duty. I beg you
to consider this only as a token of the happiness
you will confer upon me, whenever you put it in
my power to do you a good office."

The philanthropists of England take pleasure in
speaking of him: "Having become rich by com-
merce, he consecrated all his fortune to acts of benevolence. The unfortunate, without distinction of
color, had a claim on his affections. He gave to
the indigent; lent to those who could not make a
return; visited prisoners, gave them good advice,
and endeavored to bring back the guilty to *virtue.*
He died at Bridgetown, on that island, in 1758,
lamented by all, for he was a friend to all."

CAPTAIN PAUL CUFFEE.

PAUL CUFFEE, the subject of this narrative, was
the youngest son of John Cuffee, a poor African
slave; but who, by good conduct, faithfulness, and
a persevering industry, in time obtained his freedom. He afterward purchased a farm, and having
married an Indian woman, brought up a family of
ten children respectably, on one of the Elizabeth
Islands, near New Bedford, Massachusetts.

In the year 1773, when Paul was about fourteen
years of age, his father died, leaving a widow with
six daughters to the care of him and his brothers.

Although he had no learning except what he had received from the hand of friendship, yet by that means he advanced to a considerable degree of knowledge in arithmetic and navigation.

Of the latter, he acquired enough to enable him to command his own vessel in its voyages to many ports in the Southern States, the West Indies, England, Russia, and to Africa. The beginning of his business in this line was in an open boat; but by prudence and perseverance, he was at length enabled to obtain a good-sized schooner, then a brig, and afterward a ship. In the year 1806, he owned a ship, two brigs, and several smaller vessels, besides considerable property in houses and lands.

Feeling in early life a desire of benefiting his fellow-men, he made use of such opportunities as were in his power for that purpose. Hence, during the severity of winter, when he could not pursue his usual business in his little boat, he employed his time in teaching navigation to his own family and to the young men of the neighborhood. Even on his voyages, when opportunity offered, he instructed those under his care in that useful art.

He was so conscientious that he would not enter into any business, however profitable, that might have a tendency to injure his fellow-men; and seeing the dreadful effects of drunkenness, he would not deal in ardent spirits on that account.

In the place where he lived, there was no school; and as he was anxious that his children should obtain an education, he built a house on his own land, at his own expense, and gave his neighbors the free use of it; being satisfied in seeing it occupied for so useful and excellent a purpose.

In many parts of his history, we may discover that excellent trait of character which rendered him so eminently useful—a steady perseverance in laudable undertakings. It is only by an honest, industrious use of the means in our power that we can hope to become respectable.

His mind had long been affected with the degraded and miserable condition of his African brethren, and his heart yearning toward them, his thoughts were turned to the British settlement at Sierra Leone. In 1811, finding his property sufficient to warrant the undertaking, and believing it to be his duty to use a part of what God had given him for the benefit of his unhappy race, he embarked in his own brig, manned entirely by persons of color, and sailed to Africa, the land of his forefathers.

After he arrived at Sierra Leone, he had many conversations with the governor and principal inhabitants, and proposed to them a number of improvements. Thence he sailed to England, where he met great attention and respect; and being favored with an opportunity of opening his views to the Board of Managers of the African Institution, they cordially united with him in all his plans. This mission to Africa was undertaken at his own expense, and with the purest motives of benevolence.

He was very desirous of soon making another voyage, but was prevented by the war which took place between England and the United States. In 1815, however, he made preparations, and took on board his brig thirty-eight persons of color; and after a voyage of thirty-five days, he arrived safe at his destined port. These persons were to instruct the inhabitants of Sierra Leone in farming and the mechanic arts. His stay at this time was about two months, and when he took his leave, particularly of those whom he had brought over, it was like a father leaving his children, and with pious admonition commending them to the protection of God.

He was making arrangements for a third voyage, when he was seized with the complaint which terminated his labors and his life. He was taken ill in the winter, and died in the autumn following, 1817, in the fifty-ninth year of his age. For the benefit of his African brethren, he devoted a portion of his youthful acquisitions, of his latter time, and even the thoughts of his dying pillow.

As a private man, he was just and upright in all his dealings. He was an affectionate husband, a kind father, a good neighbor, and a faithful friend. He was pious without ostentation, and warmly attached to the principles of the Society of Friends, of which he was a member; and he sometimes expressed a few sentences in their Meetings, which gave general satisfaction. Regardless of the honors and pleasures of the world, he followed the example of his Divine Master, in going from place to place doing good, looking not for a reward from man, but from his Heavenly Father.

Thus walking in the ways of piety and usefulness, and in the enjoyment of an approving conscience, when death appeared, it found him in peace, and ready to depart. Such a calmness and serenity overspread his soul, and showed itself in his countenance, that the heart of even the reprobate might feel the wish, " Let me die the death of the righteous, and let my last end be like his."

A short time before he expired, feeling sensible that his end was near, he called his family together. It was an affecting and solemn scene. His wife and children, with several other relations, being assembled around him, he reached forth his feeble hand, and after embracing them all, and giving them some pious advice, he commended them to the mercy of God, and bid them a final farewell.

After this, his mind seemed almost entirely occupied with the eternal world. To one of his neighbors who came to visit him, he said, "Not many days hence, and ye shall see the glory of God. I know that my works are gone to judgment before me; but it is all well, it is all well."

He lived the life, and died the death of a Christian. He is gone whence he never shall return, and where he shall no more contend with raging billows and with howling storms. His voyages are all over, he has made his last haven, and it is that of eternal repose. Thither, could we follow him, we should learn the importance of fulfilling our duty to our Creator, to ourselves, and to our fellow-creatures.

Such was his reputation for wisdom and integrity, that his neighbors consulted him in all their important concerns; and what an honor to the son of a poor African slave! And the most respectable men in Great Britain and America were not ashamed to seek him for counsel and advice.

Thus we see how his persevering industry and economy, with the blessing of Providence, procured him wealth; his wisdom, sobriety, integrity, and good conduct made him many friends; his zealous labors for the honor of his Maker, and for the benefit of his fellow-men, gave him a peaceful conscience; and an unshaken belief in the mercies and condescending love of his Heavenly Father, afforded, in his dying moments, that calmness, serenity, and peaceful joy, which are a foretaste of immortal bliss.

The following is an extract from his address to his brethren at Sierra Leone:—" Beloved friends and fellow-countrymen, I earnestly recommend to you the propriety of assembling yourselves together to worship the Lord your God. God is a Spirit, and they that worship Him acceptably, must worship in spirit and in truth.

"Come, my African brethren, let us walk in the light of the Lord; in that pure light which bringeth salvation into the world. I recommend sobriety and steadfastness, that so professors may be good examples in all things. I recommend that early care be taken to instruct the youth while their minds are tender, that so they may be preserved from the corruptions of the world, from profanity, intemperance, and bad company.

"May servants be encouraged to discharge their duty with faithfulness ; may they be brought up to industry ; and may their minds be cultivated for the reception of the good seed which is promised to all who seek it. I want that we should be faithful in all things, that so we may become a people giving satisfaction to those who have borne the burden and heat of the day in liberating us from a state of slavery.

"I leave you in the hands of Him who is able to preserve you through time, and crown you with that blessing which is prepared for all who are faithful to the end." This appears to be the simple expression of his feelings, and the language of his heart.

When you have read this account of your brother Paul Cuffee, pause and reflect. Do not think because you cannot be as extensively useful as he was, that you cannot do any good. There are very few people, if any, in the world who cannot be useful in some way or other. If you have health, you may, by your industry, sobriety, and economy, make yourselves and your families comfortable.

By your honesty and good conduct, you may set them and your neighbors a good example. If you have aged parents, you may soothe and comfort their declining years. If you have children, you may instruct them in piety and virtue, and in such business as will

procure them a comfortable subsistance, and prepare
them for usefulness in the world.

SOLOMON BAYLEY.

In the narrative of his own life, Solomon Bayley
says: " The Lord tried to teach me His fear when I
was a little boy; but I delighted in vanity and foolish-
ness, and went astray; but He found out a way to
overcome me, and to cause me to desire His favor and
His great help; and although I thought no one could
be more unworthy of His favor, yet He did look on
me, and pity me in my great distress.

" I was born a slave in the State of Delaware, and
was one of those that were carried out of Delaware
into the State of Virginia; the laws of Delaware did
say, that slaves carried out of that State should be
free; and I asserted my right to freedom, for which
I was put on board of a vessel and sent to Richmond,
where I was put in jail, and in irons, and thence sent
in a wagon back into the country.

" On the third day after we left Richmond, in the
bitterness of my heart, I was induced to say, 'I am
past all hope;' but it pleased the Father of mercy
to look upon me, and He sent a strengthening
thought into my heart—that He that made the
heavens and the earth was able to deliver me.   I
looked up to the sky, and then on the trees and the

ground, and I believed, in a moment, that if He
could make all these, He was able to deliver me.

"Then did that Scripture come into my mind,
'They that trust in the Lord shall never be confounded.' I believed it, and got out of the wagon
unperceived, and went into the bushes. There were
three wagons in company : when they missed me,
they looked round some time for me, but not finding
me, they went on ; and that night I travelled
through thunder, lightning, and rain, a considerable
distance."

His trials and difficulties in getting along were
many and various ; but at Petersburg he met a
man from his neighborhood, circumstanced like himself : they got a small boat, went down James River,
and landed on the eastern shore of Chesapeake Bay,
and travelled to Hunting Creek, where their wives
were. "But," says he, "we found little or no satisfaction, for we were hunted like partridges on the
mountains."

His poor companion, being threatened again with
slavery, in attempting to escape, was pursued and
killed ; on which Solomon makes the following remarks : "Now, reader, you have heard of the end
of my fellow-sufferer, but I remain as yet a monu-
ment of mercy, thrown up and down on life's tempestuous sea ; sometimes feeling an earnest desire to
go away and be at rest ; but I travail on, in hopes
of overcoming at my last combat.

"It being thought best for me to leave Virginia,

J. went to Dover, in Delaware, the distance of about one hundred and twenty miles." By travelling in the night, and laying by in the day-time, he at length reached that place, but not without great difficulty, from being hunted and pursued.

In concluding this part of his narrative, he says, "Oh, what pains God takes to help His otherwise helpless creatures! Oh, that His kindness and care were more considered and laid to heart! and then there would not be that cause to complain that 'the ox knoweth his owner, and the ass his master's crib, but Israel doth not know, my people doth not consider;' but they would see that they are of more value than many sparrows; and that they are not their own, but bought with a price. Now, unto the King immortal, invisible, the only wise God, be glory and honor, dominion and power, now and forever. Amen."

In the second part of his narrative, he proceeds by remarking, "Seventh month, 24th, 1799, I got to Camden, where my master soon came from Virginia and found me, though he had not seen me since he put me on board the back-country wagon, nearly three or four hundred miles from Camden. Upon first sight, he asked me what I was going to do. I said, 'Now, master, I have suffered a great deal, and seen a great deal of trouble; I think you might let me go for little or nothing.' He said, 'I won't do that; but if you will give me forty pounds bond and good security, you may be free.'"

After much conversation between them on the subject of his right to freedom, he continues: "Finally, he sold my time˜for eighty dollars, and I went to work, and worked it out in a shorter time than he gave me, and then I was a free man. And when I came to think that the *yoke was off my neck*, and *how* it was *taken* off, I was made to wonder and admire, and to adore the order of kind Providence, which assisted me in all my way."

Here he very feelingly recites the trials and exercises of mind that attended him for not adhering to that wisdom and goodness of his Creator, which had been so marvellously manifested for his deliverance, and then proceeds to relate the circumstances respecting his wife and children. "My wife was born a slave, and remained one until she was thirty-two years of age; when her master, falling out with her, proposed sending her, with my eldest daughter, about three months old, into the back country.

"To go with her, I knew not where, or to buy her at his price, brought me to a stand; but, by the pleading of his wife and little daughter, he agreed to let me have her for one hundred and thirty-three dollars and a third, which is thirty-one pounds Virginia money. I paid what money I had saved since paying for my own freedom, and the rest as I earned it, and she was manumitted. But I had one child in bondage, my only son, and having worked through the purchase of myself and wife, I thought I would give up my son to the ordering of Divine Providence.

" So we worked and rented land, and got along twelve or thirteen years, when my son's master died, and his property had to be sold, and my son among the rest, at public sale. The backwoods-men having come over and given such large prices for slaves, it occasioned a great concern to come over my mind, and I told it to many of my friends, and they all encouraged me to buy him, but I told them I could have no heart to do it, because at his master's death he was appraised at four hundred dollars; however, I went to the sale. When the crier said, ' A likely young negro-fellow for sale,' and then asked for a bid, I said, ' Two hundred dollars.'

" As soon as I made this bid, a man that I feared would sell him to the backwoods-men, bid three hundred and thirty-three dollars, which beat down all my courage, but a thought struck me—Don't give out so—and I bid one shilling, but they continued to bid until they got him up to three hundred and sixty dollars, and I thought I could do no more; but those men who had engaged to be my securities, encouraged me, and some young men who were present, and had their hearts touched with a feeling for my distress, said, ' Solomon, if you will make one more bid, we will give you five dollars apiece;' so I turned round and said, ' One shilling;' so he was knocked off to me at three hundred and sixty dollars and a shilling : this was in the year 1813. •

" Then I believed that God would work, and none could hinder Him, and that a way would be made

for me, though I knew not how; and I confess the
eyes of my mind appeared to be dazzled as I was
let into a sight of the great goodness of the Highest
in undertaking for me; but I felt a fear lest my behavior should not be suitable to the kindness and
favor shown toward me.

"Oh, that all men would study the end of their
creation, and act accordingly! Then they would walk
in the light of His countenance indeed, and 'in His
name rejoice all the day, and in His righteousness
for ever be exalted.'

> ' Then should their sun in smiles decline,
> And bring a peaceful night ; '

which may all who read these lines, desire, and seek,
and obtain, through Jesus Christ our Lord.   Amen."

In the account of his mother, he says, " She was
born of a woman brought from Guinea about the year
1690, then about eleven years old.   She was brought
into one of the most barbarous families; and though
treated hard, she had many children, and lived to a
great age.   My mother had thirteen sons and daughters, and served the same cruel family until they died.

"Then great distress and dispersion took place.
Our young mistress married, and brought our family
out of the State of Virginia into the State of Delaware; but by their removing back to Virginia, we
were entitled to our freedom; and attempting to recover it by law, we were sold and scattered wide.

My father and two of his children were taken unaware, and sent to the West Indies. My mother was in the house at the time, but made her escape, leaving a child about eleven months old, which some kind friend carrying to her, she took, and travelling through Delaware, went into New Jersey.

"We were separated about eighteen years, except that I once visited her, and carried her seventeen or eighteen dollars, which, in my circumstances, was a sacrifice, but I was favored to find that satisfaction which I esteemed more than time or money. Being thoughtful about my mother, I sent for her to come to the State of Delaware, and when we were brought together, it was very comfortable, and we could sit and tell of the dangers and difficulties we had been brought through. She lived to a great age, and departed without much complaint, like one falling asleep.

"*An account of my eldest daughter Margaret, who died in the twenty-fourth year of her age.*

" She was a pleasant child in her manners and behavior, yet fond of gay dress and new fashions ; yet her mind was much inclined to her book, and to read good lessons ; and it pleased the Father of mercy to open her understanding to see excellent things out of His law, and to convince her that it was His will she should be holy here, and happy hereafter ; but custom, habit, and shame, seemed to chain her down, so that she appeared like one halting between two opinions.

"But about a month before she was taken for death, she went to a Meeting, under a concern about her future state; and the Meeting appeared to be favored with the outpouring of the Spirit of love and of power. Margaret came home under great concern of mind, and manifested a wonderful change in her manners and behavior; I believe the whole family were affected at the sight of the alteration, which indeed appeared like that of the prodigal son coming home to his father. For my own part, I felt fear and great joy—such was her delight to read the Bible and ask the meaning of certain texts of Scripture, which evidenced a concern to make sure work for eternity.

"In this frame of mind she was taken for death. She appeared very desirous to live, for the first four weeks; but was very patient, and of a sweet temper and disposition all the time. I recollect but one instance when she was known to give way to peevish fretfulness; then I, feeling the evil spirit striving to get the advantage of her, very tenderly and earnestly admonished her not to regard trifles, but to look to that Power which was able to save her; and from that time she became passive and resigned.

"The following two weeks her pain was great, and baffled all the force of medicine. A few days before her departure, she was urged with much brokenness of heart to make confession, when she was let into a view of the vanity of the world, with all its glitter-

ing snares, and said she could not rest till her hair
was cut off; for, she said, ' I was persuaded to plait
my hair against my father's advice, and I used to tie
up my head when father would come to see me, and
hide ruffles and gay dress from him, and now I cannot rest till my hair is cut off.' I said, ' No, my
daughter, let it be till thee gets well.' She answered,
' Oh, no, cut it now.' So I, to pacify her, took and
cropped it.

"After this, she appeared filled with raptures of
joy, and talked of going, as if death had lost its sting.
This was about three days before her departure; and
she seemed to have her senses as long as she could
speak. A little before her speech left her, she called
us all, one by one, held out her hand, bade us farewell, and looked as if she felt that assurance and
peace that destroy the fear of death ; and while she
held out her hands, she earnestly charged us to meet
her in heaven.

" I desire now to give the pious a brief account of
the life and death of my youngest daughter, Leah
Bayley, who departed this life the 27th of 7th month,
1821, aged twenty-one years and six months. She,
from a child, was more weakly and sickly than her
sister Margaret, and the thought of leaving her here
in this ill-natured world, caused me many serious
moments; but the great Parent of all good, in the
greatness of IIis care, took her away, and relieved me
of the care of her forever.

" Weakness of body and mind appeared in her as

she grew up, and an inclination to vanity and idleness; but being bound out under an industrious mistress, to learn to work and to have schooling, her mind soon became much inclined to her book and then to business. Her school-mistress gave her a little book concerning some pious young people that lived happily, and died happily, and were gone to heaven; namely,—

" Young Samuel, that little child
Who served the Lord, lived undefiled.
Like young Abijah I must be,
That good things may be found in me.
Young Timothy, that blessed youth
Who sought the Lord and loved the truth.
I must not sin as others do,
Lest I lie down in sorrow too. ·

" These blessed examples won her heart so as to bury every other enjoyment; she seemed to possess as great a deadness to the world as any young woman I ever observed. She seemed not ashamed to read in any company, white or colored; and she read to the sick with intense desire, which appeared from her weeping and solid manner of behavior. She seemed to desire to walk in the fear of the Lord all the day long; and every body that observed her remarked her serious, steady behavior.

" She seemed as if she was trying to imitate those good children whom she read about; and so continued until she was taken sick; and though her sickness was long and sharp, yet she bore it like a lamb. A few days before her decease, I was noticing how hard she drew her breath; she looked very wistful at me, and said, 'Oh, father! how much I do suffer!' I answered, 'Yes, my dear, I believe thee does.'

"Then, after a long pause, she said, 'But I think I never shall say I suffer too much.' This, I apprehended, was extorted from a view of the sufferings of Christ and her own imperfections. The day she died, she called us all, one by one, and, like her sister Margaret, held out her hand, and with much composure of mind bade us farewell, as if she was only going a short walk, and to return."

The last accounts from Solomon Bayley say, that he was very diligent and faithful in his calling—laboring not only for the souls of his brethren, but for their bodies also—by setting them the best example he was capable of, in cultivating his land to the best advantage, and by improving his plans, to show the natives, as well as the emigrants, the usefulness and comforts of civilized life.

CLARINDA,

A PIOUS COLORED WOMAN OF SOUTH CAROLINA, WHO DIED AT THE AGE OF A HUNDRED AND TWO YEARS.

THE subject of this memoir was brought up in a state of ignorance unworthy of a Christian country; and following the propensities of a corrupt heart, she was, by her own confession, "sold under sin," and involved in almost every species of iniquity. And for the furtherance of her wicked designs, she learned to play on the violin, and usually, on the first day of the week, sallied forth with her instrument, in order to draw persons of both sexes together, who, not having the fear of God before their eyes, delighted, like herself, in sinful and pernicious amusements, which keep the soul from God and the heart from repentance.

But even on these occasions she found it difficult to struggle against the Spirit of the Most High. Often was it sounded in her conscience, " Clarinda, God ought not to be slighted—God ought not to be forgotten ; " but these monitions were treated with derision, and in the hardness of her heart she would exclaim : " Go, you fool, I do not know God—go, I do not wish to know Him."

On one occasion, while on her way to a dance, these blasphemous thoughts, in answer to the monitions of conscience, were passing through her mind, and in this frame she reached the place of appointment, and mingled in the gay throng. While participating in the dance, she was seized with fits, and convulsively fell to the ground. From that moment, she lost her love of dancing, and no more engaged in this vain amusement.

She did not, however, forsake the evil of her ways, but continued her course of wickedness. Thus she went on for about twenty years, when she lost her only child, and was confined for several months by severe illness. During this period of bodily suffering, her mind was brought under awful convictions for sin : she perceived that the great Jehovah is a sin-hating and sin-avenging God, and that He will by no means clear the guilty.

She remained in a distressed state of mind for about three months, and when a little bodily strength was restored, she sought solitary places, where she poured out her soul unto the Lord, and in His own good time He spoke peace to her wounded spirit. One day being thus engaged in earnest prayer, and looking unto the Lord for deliverance, the evening approached unregarded, her soul was deeply humbled, and the night passed in prayer, while rivers of tears (to use her own expressive language) ran down her cheeks, and she ceased not to implore mercy from Him who is able to bind up the broken-hearted.

While thus engaged, and all this time ignorant of her Saviour, something whispered to her mind, "Ask in the name of Christ." She queried, "Who is Christ?" and in reply, these passages of Scripture seemed repeated to her : "Let not your heart be troubled; ye believe in God, believe also in Me." "In My Father's house are many mansions: I go to prepare a place for you, that where I am there ye may be also." "I am the way, the truth, and the life; no man cometh unto the Father but by Me."

Being desirous to know whence these impressions proceeded, she was led to believe that they were received through the influence of the Holy Spirit. This

remarkable passage was also presented to her mind :
" Therefore, being justified by faith, we have peace
with God through our Lord and Saviour Jesus Christ."

She now felt the love of God shed abroad in her
heart ; the overwhelming burden of sin was removed,
and she received ability to sing praises to the Lord on
the banks of deliverance.

Having been thus permitted to see the desire of her
soul, she was anxious to learn more of the divine will,
and inquired, like the apostle, " Lord, what wilt Thou
have me to do ? " and like him she was commanded to
be a witness of what she had seen and heard. Believing she had a commission given her to preach the
Gospel, she began to warn the sinful and licentious,
that they must crucify the man of sin, or for ever
forego the hope of salvation.

This raised her a host of enemies, both white and
colored ; and she underwent, many years, cruelty and
persecution which could hardly obtain credence. She
bore about on her body the visible marks of her faithful allegiance to the Lord Jesus ; yet, while alluding
to this, tears filled her eyes, and she said with emotion,
" I am thankful that I have been found worthy to suffer for my blessed Saviour."

Although living in great poverty, and subsisting at
times on casual charity, with health impaired by the
sufferings through which she had passed, yet neither
promises of protection, accompanied with the offer of
the good things of this life, on the one hand, nor the
dreadful persecution she endured on the other, could

make her relinquish the office of a minister of the Gospel.

This office she continued to exercise, holding meetings regularly on the first day of the week, at her own little habitation, where a greater number at times assembled than could be accommodated in the house. It may be interesting to add some particulars relative to the trial of her faith and the persecution she suffered.

One individual in whose neighborhood she lived, who was much annoyed by hearing her sing and pray, offered, if she would desist, to provide her with a home and the comforts of life ; but she replied, she had received a commission to preach the Gospel, and she would preach it as long as she had breath. Several ill-intentioned persons one night surrounded her house, and commanded her to come out to them. This she refused to do. After threatening her for some time, they forced open the door, and having seized their victim, they beat her cruelly, so that her head was deeply indented with the blows she received.

At another time she was so much injured that she was left nearly lifeless on the open road, whither she had fled to escape from them ; but her unsuccessful efforts increased the rage of her pursuers, and after treating her with the utmost barbarity, they left her. She was found after some time, but so exhausted by the loss of blood that she was unable to walk, and from the effects of that cruelty she did not recover for years. But it may be said of her, that she joyfully bore persecution for Christ's sake.

A man who lived in the same village, being much incensed at the undaunted manner in which she stood forth as a minister of the meek and crucified Saviour, swore that he would beat her severely if ever he found an opportunity. One evening, as she was walking home on a solitary road, she saw this person riding towards her. She knew his intentions, and from his character she did not doubt that he would execute them.

She trembled from head to foot, escape seemed impracticable, and prayer was her only refuge. As he advanced, she observed that his handkerchief fell and was wafted by the wind to a little distance. She picked it up, he stopped his horse, and she handed it to him in a submissive manner; he looked at her fiercely for a moment, when his countenance softened; he took it, saying, " Well, Clarinda," and passed on.

She was not able to read a word till her sixty-sixth year, but she was in the practice of getting persons to read the Holy Scriptures to her, much of which she retained in her memory with remarkable accuracy. By dint of application, she was at length able to read them herself; and those who visited her in advanced life, found her knowledge of the Scriptures, as well as her growth in grace, very surprising.

When she was one hundred years old, and very feeble, she would, if able to get out of bed, on the Sabbath morning, discharge what she thought to be her duty, by conversing with and exhorting both the white and colored people who came to her house, often standing for half an hour at a time. Her zeal was indeed great, and her faith steadfast.

She said she often wished she could write, that she might in this way also express her anxiety for the good of souls. Then she would have described more of the exercises of her mind upon the depravity of man by nature and by practice, with the unbounded and redeeming love and mercy of God through Jesus Christ.

The person who gives the account of Clarinda's death, says, " I was prevented from seeing her often in her last moments ; when I did see her she was always the same—her one theme the love of God to poor sinners, which was always her style of speaking. One day, as I sat by her bedside, she said to me, ' Do you think I am a Christian ? ' ' Yes,' I answered, ' I do believe you are a Christian.' ' I have tried to be,' she replied, ' but now that I suffer in my body, when I think what an unprofitable servant I have been, I am distressed.' She then wept. ' You know,' I said, ' it is not how *much* we can do, but what we do *sincerely* for the love of Christ, that is acceptable.' She seemed comforted, and talked as usual.

"She showed me much affection when I left her, saying, ' I shall not live long, my dear ———,' and, adding a few other words, blessed me, and bid me pray for her. She had frequently expressed her fears of the bodily sufferings of death, but not accompanied with a dread of eternal death. I asked her, when she was ill, if she *now* feared to die. She said ' No ; this fear was taken away some time previous to my illness.' "

She requested that her people, as she called them, might continue to meet at her house, but this was not allowed. I am told they sometimes meet elsewhere, and are called "Clarinda's People." When dying, she told those near her to follow her *only* as she had followed Christ. Her death occurred in 1832. "Those that be planted in the house of the Lord shall flourish in the courts of our God. They shall bring forth fruit in old age."

While perusing this remarkable account of "a brand plucked from the burning," let those who from their earliest years have enjoyed the inestimable privilege of access to the sacred volume, and various other religious means, seriously consider the blessed Saviour's words : " Unto whomsoever much is given, of him shall be much required."

NAIMBANNA.

WHEN the Sierra Leone Company was first settled, they endeavored to bring over to their friendship all the petty African princes in their neighborhood. Among others, they applied to a chief of the name of Naimbanna, who was remarkable for a good disposition and an acute understanding. He easily saw that the intention of the company was friendly to Africa, and entered into amity with them.

They spoke to him about the slave trade, and gave him reasons for wishing to have it abolished. He was convinced of its wickedness, and declared that not one of his subjects should ever go into slavery again. By degrees, they began to talk to him about religion, but he was rather wary on that head. It seems he had formed some prejudices against Christianity.

Finding, however, that the Company's factory contained a very good sort of people, and that they lived happily among themselves, he began to think more favorably of their religion; but he was still backward either in receiving it himself, or in making it the religion of his country. He was well convinced of the barbarous state of his own people, on a comparison with Europeans, and he wished for nothing more than a reformation among them, especially in religion.

But as he found there were several kinds (or forms) of religion in the world, he wished to know which was the best before he introduced either of them. To ascertain this point as well as he could, he took the following method: He sent one of his sons into Turkey, among the Mohammedans; a second into Portugal, among the Papists; and the third he recommended to the Sierra Leone Company, desiring they would send him to England, to be there instructed in the religion of that country.

It appears he meant to be directed by the reports
of his sons in the choice of a national religion. Of
the two former of these young men, we have no particulars, only that one of them became very vicious.
The last mentioned, though I believe the eldest, bore
his father's name, Naimbanna. The Sierra Leone
Company received the charge of him with great
pleasure, believing that nothing could have a better
effect in promoting their benevolent schemes, than
making him a good Christian.

Young Naimbanna was a perfect African in form,
and had the features with which the African face is
commonly marked. While he was with the Company, he seemed a well-disposed tractable youth; but
when opposed, he was impatient, fierce, and subject
to violent passion. In the first ship that sailed he
was sent to England, where he arrived in the year
1791.

We may imagine with what astonishment he surveyed every object that came before him : but his
curiosity, in prudent hands, became, from the first
the medium of useful instruction. During his voyage
he acquired some knowledge of the English language;
and although he could not speak it with any degree
of fluency, he could understand much of what he
heard spoken, which greatly facilitated his learning it,
when he applied to it in a more regular way.

The difficulty of learning to speak and read being in
a great degree subdued, he was put upon the grand
point for which he was sent to England—that of being

instructed in the Christian religion. The gentlemen to whose care he had been recommended, alternately took him under their protection; and each gave up his whole time to him, faithfully discharging the trust which he had voluntarily, and without any emolument, undertaken.

Naimbanna was first made acquainted with the value of the Bible; the most material parts of the Old Testament, as well as the New, were explained to him. The great necessity of a Saviour, for the sinfulness of man, was pointed out; the end and design of Christianity, its doctrines, its precepts, and its sanctions, were all made intelligible to him. With a clearness of understanding which astonished those who took the care of instructing him, he made those divine truths familiar to his mind. He received the Gospel with joy, and carried it home to his heart as the means of happiness both in this world and the next.

His love for reading the Scriptures, and hearing them read, was such that he never was tired of the exercise. Every other part of learning that he was put upon, as arithmetic, for instance, was heavy work with him, and he soon began to complain of fatigue; but even when he was most fatigued, if he was asked to read in the Bible, he was always ready, and generally expressed his readiness by some emotions of joy.

In short, he considered the Bible as the rule which was to direct his life; and he made a real use of every piece of instruction which he obtained from it. This was evident in all his actions. If his behavior was at any time wrong, and a passage of Scripture was shown to him, which forbade such behavior, whatever it was, he instantly complied with the rule he received. Of this there were many instances.

One related to dress. He had a little vanity about him, was fond of finery, admired it in other people, and was always ready to adorn himself. His kind instructors told him these were childish inclinations; that decency and propriety of dress are pleasing, but that foppery is disgusting. Above all, they told him that the Christian is ordered to be " clothed with humility, and to put on the ornament of a meek and quiet spirit." Such passages, whenever they were suggested to him, checked all the little vanities of his heart, and made him ashamed of what he had just before so eagerly desired.

The irritable passions, where lay his weakest side, were conquered in the same way. His friends once carried him to the House of Commons, to hear a debate on the slave trade, which Colonel Tarlton defended with some warmth. When Naimbanna came out of the house, he exclaimed, with great vehemence and indignation, that he would kill that man where-ever he met him; for he told stories of his country. He told people that his countrymen would not work, and that was a great story. His countrymen would work; but Englishmen would not buy work; they would buy only men.

His friends told him that he should not be angry

with Colonel Tarlton, for perhaps he had been misin
formed, and knew no better. Besides, they told him
that, at any rate, he had no right to kill him : for the
Almighty says, " Vengeance is mine, I will repay,
saith the Lord." This calmed him in a moment;
and he never afterward expressed the least indignation toward Colonel Tarlton ; but he would have
been ready to show him any friendly office if it had
fallen in his way.

At another time, when he saw a drayman using his
horse ill, he became enraged, and declared he would
get a gun and shoot that fellow directly. But his
anger was presently assuaged by this or some similar
passage of Scripture : " Be ye angry, and sin not ; let
not the sun go down upon your wrath." He showed
so much tenderness of conscience that he seemed anxious about nothing but to know what his religion
required him to do.

When he could determine the rectitude of an action,
he set an example even to Christians, by showing that
he thought there was no difficulty in the performance.
He said his father had ordered him, when he arrived
in England, never to drink more at one time than a
single glass of wine ; and he considered his father's
injunction as sacred. On this head, therefore, all the
instruction which he wanted was to turn his temperance into a Christian virtue, by practising it with a
sincere desire to please God.

In the gay scenes which often presented themselves
to his view, he never mixed. His friends were very

solicitous to keep him from all dissipation, which might have corrupted the beautiful simplicity of mind that was so characteristic in him. He was fond of riding on horseback, but when he got upon a horse, it was difficult to govern his desire for rapid motion. After remaining in England a year and a half, and being carefully instructed in the Christian religion, he only waited for an opportunity of returning home, which . did not occur for five or six months afterward.

In the meantime, two great points were the burden of his thoughts, and gave him much distress. The first related to his father, whose death he heard had happened about a year after he left the country. The principal cause of his solicitude was his uncertainty whether his father had died a Christian. He knew that he had been well disposed toward Christianity, but he had never heard whether he had fully embraced it.

His other difficulty regarded himself. He had now attained the end at which he had aimed. He had been instructed in a religion which he was convinced would promote the happiness of his people if it could be established among them. But how was that to be done? With regard to himself, he had had wise and learned men to instruct him. But what could his abilities do in such a work—especially considering the wild and savage manners of his countrymen? In every light, the greatness of the attempt perplexed him.

With a mind distressed by these difficulties, he took an affectionate leave of his kind friends in England, and embarked for Africa in one of the Company's ships, which was named after him, the Naimbanna. Though he had shown great affection for his own country and relations, yet the kindness which he had received from his friends in England had impressed him strongly; and it was not without a great struggle that he broke away from them at last.

The distress he felt was increased by the society he mixed in at sea—being very different from that which he had left behind. The profligate manners and licentious language of the ship's company shocked him exceedingly. The purity of his mind could not bear it. He had hoped, that in a Christian country he should always find himself among Christians, but he was greatly disappointed.

The company he was in appeared to him as ignorant and uninformed as his own countrymen, and much less innocent in their manners. At length, the oaths and abominable conversation which he continually heard, affected him so much that he complained to the captain of the ship, and desired him to put a stop to so indecent language. The captain endeavored to check it, but with little effect, which gave Naimbanna increased distress.

But still the great burden of his mind, was the difficulty which he foresaw in the attempt to introduce Christianity among his countrymen. Many were the schemes he thought of; but insuperable obstacles seemed to arise on every side. All this perplexity, which his active and generous' mind underwent, recoiled upon himself.

His thoughts were continually on the stretch, and this, it was supposed, at length occasioned a fever, which seized him when his voyage was nearly at an end. His malady increasing, it was attended with delirium, which left him only a few lucid intervals. In these, his mind always shone out full of religious hope and patient resignation to the will of God.

In one of these intervals, he told Mr. Graham, a fellow-passenger with whom he was most intimate, that he began to think he should be called away before he had an opportunity to tell·his mother of the mercies of God toward him, and of his obligations to the Sierra Leone Company. He then desired him to write his will, which he began in the presence of Captain Wooles and James Cato, a servant that attended Naimbanna.

When Mr. Graham had written a considerable part, as particularly directed, manifesting the feelings and generosity of his heart, Naimbanna complained of fatigue, and said he would finish it after he had taken a little rest. But his fever came on with increased violence, and his delirium scarcely ever left him afterward.

The night after, the vessel, though close to the African coast, durst not attempt to land, as the wind was contrary, and there was danger of running on the Scarries bank. Next morning, though the wind con-

tinued contrary, Mr. Graham went off to the settlement in an open boat to procure medical aid. But
when the physician came on board, Naimbanna was
just alive; and in that state he was carried to the
settlement, the next morning, July 17th, 1793, when
the ship came to anchor.

On the first account of his illness, an express was
sent to inform his friends at Robanna; and soon after
he was landed, his mother, brothers, sisters, and relatives came to the settlement. The distracted looks
of his mother, and the wildness of his sisters' grief,
affected everyone. His cousin Henry, an ingenuous
youth, who stood among them, attracted the attention
of all by the solemn sorrow of his countenance, which
seemed to discover a heart full of tenderness and woe.
In the meantime, the dying youth appeared every
moment drawing nearer the close of life.

His voice failing more and more, the little he said
was with difficulty understood. Once or twice, those
who stood around him caught hold of something like
our Saviour's words: "Many are called, but few
chosen." About an hour before he died, his voice
wholly failed. He was awhile restless and uneasy,
till, turning his head on his pillow, he found an easier
posture, and lay perfectly quiet.

About seven in the evening of the day on which he
was brought on shore, he expired without a groan.
When his mother and other relatives found his
breath was gone, their shrieks and agonizing cries
were distressing beyond measure. Instantly, in a

kind of frantic madness, they snatched up his body, hurried it into a canoe, and went off with it to Robanna. Some of the gentlemen of the factory immediately followed in boats, with a coffin.

When the corpse was laid decently into it, Mr. Horne, the clergyman, read the funeral service over it, amid a number of people, and finished with an extempore prayer. The ceremony was conducted with so much solemnity, and performed in so affecting a manner, that the impression was communicated throughout the whole crowd. They drew closer and closer, as Mr. Horne continued to speak ; and though they understood not a syllable of what he said, they listened to him with great attention, and bore witness, with every mark of sorrow, to the powers of sympathy.

After the ceremony was over, the gentlemen of the factory retired to their boats, leaving the corpse, as his friend desired, to be buried according to the custom of the country.

ZILPAH MONTJOY.

In the year 1821, died, in the city of New York, an aged woman of color, named Zilpah Montjoy ; whose pious circumspect life rendered her an object of peculiar interest to many of her acquaintances ; to some of these, whose friendly notice she had experi-

enced, she more than once related the following circumstance :—

Being a slave, inured to hard labor, she was
brought up in such extreme ignorance as to have no
idea that she was an accountable being—that there
was a future state—not even that death was universal, until the sixteenth year of her age, when a girl of
her own color dying in the neighborhood, she was
permitted to attend the funeral.

The minister's text was, " Man that is born of a
woman is of few days and full of trouble : he cometh
forth like a flower, and is cut down: he fleeth also as
a shadow, and continueth not ! " by which and subse-
quent remarks, she understood that all were to die ;
that there was a state of existence after death, a preparation for which was necessary while here.

She was much affected, and returned home in great
agitation.   Revolving these things in her mind for
several days, she at length asked her mistress whether
she had understood right, that all must die.   The reply was, " Go to your work."   She continued thus
exercised for a considerable time, earnestly desiring
to know what she had to do, but had no one to give
her instruction.

In this tried state, the Lord was pleased to reveal
Himself, and impress on her untaught mind a belief
in an omnipotent and omniscient Being, and that His
law was written on the heart.   Thus, gradually becoming calm and settled, her confidence was made
strong in Him, who, hiding His counsels from the wise

and prudent in their own eyes, "hath revealed them unto babes." And it is believed she was from that time guarded and careful in her conduct.

She married, and had two daughters, one of whom was taken at an early age, and placed at so great a distance from her that she never saw her after. The other died when about grown, and being also bereaved of her husband, she was very lonely. But under these trials she appears to have been sustained, as was David when he could say, "Thy rod and thy staff they comfort me."

She was a member of the Methodist Church, and a diligent attender of their meetings as long as her strength permitted. When she was (as near as can be ascertained) about sixty-eight years old, the Clarkson Association for teaching colored women to read and write was established.

And when she received the information, she offered herself as a scholar, but the teachers endeavored to dissuade her, telling her she was too old to begin, as she did not know a letter, and her sight was so impaired as to require two pairs of spectacles; she however urged admittance, stating that her only motive was a desire to be able to read the Bible, and she believed " the Lord would help her," adding, " We are never too old to do good."

And being admitted, she was very diligent in her attendance, and by great perseverance became able to read a little in the New Testament; and one with large print being given her, she prized it very highly, and would frequently open it and read one of the chapters contained in Christ's sermon on the mount, calling it " the blessed chapter."

But notwithstanding her great desire to learn, she did not allow her studies to interfere with her religious engagements; and the time for meeting with her class being fixed on one of the afternoons that the school was taught, it was inconvenient to her; but as the school commenced at three o'clock, and the meeting at four, the hour between she generally spent at the school, staying as long as it would do, and then going as quickly as she could, to be punctual to the time. Sometimes she has been seen running, when she heard the clock strike and found herself a little too late.

She was industrious and frugal, but liberated late in life, she barely procured a subsistence; and for the last two or three years, being nearly past labor, she was dependent on the benevolence of others : but at no time, however destitute and tried, did she lose her confidence in the power of Him " who provideth for the raven his food," often saying at such seasons, " The Lord has been my helper, and I trust in Him." And when any favor was conferred on her, she feelingly expressed her gratitude, yet mostly with reference to the Great Supreme, for giving her friends so kind.

At a certain time, a friend, being unusually thoughtful about her, went to see how she was situated, taking with her a loaf of bread. She found her unable to go out, and without provision ; and querying with

her, " Zilpah, art thou here alone ?" she replied,
" No, I am never alone ; my Master is with me. When
I awake in the night season he talks with me. He
has promised to take care of me, and He has done it;
He has now sent me that loaf of bread." At another
time, she said to a person who visited her, " How good
the Lord is ; I have always something to eat, for if I
take my last morsel, some one comes and brings me
more before I want again."

Her understanding failed, so that for several weeks
before her death she know very little ; but her conversation was innocent, sometimes saying, " If it is
the Lord's will to take me, I am willing to go, but I
must wait His time." And He was pleased to release
her, after a short confinement, without any apparent
disease but the decline of nature, about the seventy-
ninth year of her age.

BELINDA LUCAS.

A woman of color, living in Chrystie street, New
York, is now, 1825, about one hundred years old.
She retains her faculties remarkably well, and she recently gave the following account of herself: " When
I was a small child in Africa, being one day at play
in the woods, some people came along ; one of whom
catched me, and throwing me over his shoulder, ran
away with me. After he had gone some distance, he
put me down and whipped me to make me run.

" When we came to the water, they put me into the

ship and carried me to Antigua. Soon after, the captain of a vessel from New York, taking a liking to me, bought me, and brought me here. I was then so little, that I slept sometimes at my mistress's feet. I think there was only one house for worship in the city then ; and I remember very well that up Broadway there were only a few small houses; and where the college (in Park Place) stands it was woods.

"I was sold several times, married twice, and had one child that died young. I was baptized in St. Paul's church, not long after it was built; and when I was about forty years old, I bought my freedom for twenty pounds. Not long after I married my last husband, I paid for his freedom, and we went to Charleston. After living there about seven years, he died; and knowing I had many friends and acquaintances in New York, I came back.

"I brought a hundred dollars with me, which I put into the church stock. From that I have received seven dollars every year, and with it I buy my winter firewood. By working early and late, besides my day's work, I earned money, and got a life lease of this spot of ground, and built this house; and in this room" (which is on the first floor) "I have lived many years.

"The upper part I rent; but sometimes the people have been poor, and could not pay me; then I lost it; but these people pay me very well. I have been asked many times to sell it, but I think it is much better for me to stay quietly here than to be moving

about: and besides, I let Mr. —— have fifty dollars, and when he failed, I lost it; and the bad folks
have several times taken money out of my chest; and
I was afraid, if I did sell, I should lose that also, and
then I should be very bad off.

"As I have no relation of my own, when I am
gone, and don't want these things any more, they are
to be divided among my husband's folks." A person
present told her she should have a writing drawn, to
tell how they should be divided; saying, "Perhaps
they will quarrel about it." She said, "I have told
them if they did, them that quarrelled must not have
anything."

When asked if she could read, she answered, "Yes;
when I was young I learned to spell a little, but I did
not know how to put the words together, till I went
to the Clarkson school. There I learned to read; and
though I can't read all the hard words in the Bible, I
can read Matthew and John very well." A representation of the crucifixion of Christ hanging over the
chimney-piece, she pointed to it, and explained it very
intelligibly, remarking that, "To Mary, who was
kneeling near the cross, it was said, 'Woman, behold
thy Son,' and to one of those standing by, 'Behold
thy Mother.'"

This representation appeared to afford her much
interest in contemplating it, though she looked only
to the Lord for consolation, and several times, while
giving this account, testified of His goodness and
mercy to her; saying, "It is the Lord's will that I

should be so comfortably provided for. When I was younger, and worked so steadily, the people used to say, ' Belinda, what do you work so hard for, and lay up money? you have no children to take it when you are gone.'

" I did not know then, but the Lord knew that I was to live a great while, and He put it into my heart to do so, and now I have plenty, and trouble nobody for a living. I am unwell this morning, but by and by, when I feel better, I intend to clean up. I used to live very snug and comfortable ; I can't get anybody now to put up my things for me so well as I can do it for myself." Her bed had curtains, and appeared to have comfortable covering on it. She had a looking-glass, an arm-chair, a carpet on her floor, and other necessary furniture.

She further said, " When I was able, I went often to see the sick, and the suffering poor, and do something for them, and I sometimes prayed by their bedside ; " and added, " I believe the Lord heard my prayers." Placing her hands in an attitude of supplication, and turning her eyes upward, " I often pray now, and I leave it to Him, and He gives me what I pray for. If He thinks it best for me to live longer yet, I am willing to stay ; and if He thinks best to take me away, I am ready to go."

On being asked how old she was, she replied, " When Peter Williams was going to Hayti, and he came to see me and bid me farewell, he said, ' Belinda, I have been calculating your age, as near as I can from circumstances, and I believe you are about a hundred years old.' I thought I was older, but I suppose he must be correct.

"I used to work for the rich folks, and they seemed to love me, and treated me very kindly. Mrs. T——, and Mrs. H——, and many others, have been to see me a great many times. Mr. Livingston, the lawyer, who died at Washington, you remember —with his first wife's father, Mr. Kittletas, I lived, and of him I bought my freedom. And when I went to Mr. Livingston's, he would say, ' Why, Belinda, you have a long life of it here.' I would say, ' Yes, master, the Lord knows, but I don't, why I stay so long '—but, dear man, he is gone!"

On being asked why she lived alone, she said, "If I have somebody with me, they will want other company, and that will make more noise than I like. I love to be still; then I can think. And when I am sick, the people up stairs are kind to me, and do what little I want done."

When speaking of reading, she said, I met with a bad accident lately; I dropped my spectacles in the fire, and it spoiled them: when I can get into the Bowery, to Mr. ——'s store, I can get another pair; but nobody can get them for me—they would not know how to suit my eyes—and then I always pay cash for what I get—I have found it the best way. In all my life long, there has never anybody had the scratch of a pen against me. I have been saving too: them plates there " (pointing to her closet), " I brought them with me from Charleston , before Washington's war."

In this unpolished narrative, we see the benefit of acquiring steady habits in early life—of honest, persevering industry—and frugality in the use of what was so obtained. From the one hundred dollars put into church stock, she has in fifty years received three hundred and fifty dollars; and in such a way as to be particularly useful to her. Her pious care of the sick; her quiet, decent, and comely way of living; and her exertions in learning to read, even at the advanced age of eighty years, are also worthy of particular notice.

GUSTAVUS VASSA.

TAKEN FROM HIS NARRATIVE, WRITTEN ABOUT THE
YEAR 1787.

" I OFFER here neither the history of a saint, a hero, nor a tyrant. I believe there are few events in my life, which have not happened to many; but when I compare my lot with that of many of my countrymen, I acknowledge the mercies of Providence in the occurrences that have taken place.

" That part of Africa known by the name of Guinea, to which the trade for slaves is carried on, extends along the coast above 3,400 miles, from Senegal to Angola, and includes a variety of kingdoms.

The most considerable of these is Benin, as it respects
its extent, wealth, and richness of soil.   It is bounded
on the sea 170 miles, and its interior seems only terminated by the empire of Abyssinia, near 1,500 miles
from its first boundaries.

" In one of the most remote and fertile provinces
of this kingdom I was born, in the year 1745.   As
our country is one where nature is prodigal of her
favors, our wants, which are few, are easily supplied.
All our industry is turned to the improvement of
those blessings, and we are habituated to labor from
our early years ; and by this means we have no
beggars.

" Our houses never exceed one story, and are built
of wood, thatched with reeds, and the floors are generally covered with mats.   The dress of both sexes consists of a long piece of calico or muslin, wrapped
loosely round the body ; our beds are also covered
with the same kind of cloth ; this the women make
when they are not engaged in labor with the men.
Our tillage is in a large common, and all the people
resort thither in a body and unite in the labor.

" My father being a man of rank, had a numerous
family ; his children consisted of one daughter, and
a number of sons, of which I was the youngest.   As
I generally attended my mother, she took great pains
in forming my mind, and training me to exercise.   In
this way, I grew up to about the eleventh year of my
age, when an end was put to my happiness in the following manner :

"One day, when all our people were gone to their work, and only my dear sister and myself were left to watch the house, two men and a woman came, and seizing us both, stopped our mouths that we should not make a noise, and ran off with us into the woods, where they tied our hands, and took us some distance, to a small house, where we stayed that night.

"The next morning, after keeping in the woods some distance, we came to an opening, where we saw some people at work, and I began to cry for assistance; but this made them tie us faster, and again stop our mouths; and they put me into a sack until we had got out of sight of these people. When they offered us food we could not eat. Often bathing each other in tears, our only respite was sleep; but alas! even the privilege of weeping together was soon denied us. While enclosed in each other's arms we were torn asunder, and I was left in a state of distress not to be described.

"After travelling a great distance, suffering many hardships, and being sold several times, one evening my dear sister was brought to the same house. We were both so overcome that we could not speak for some time, but clung to each other and wept. And when the people were told that we were brother and sister, they indulged us with being together; and one of the men at night lay between us, and allowed us to hold each other's hand across him.

"This comfort, small as it may appear to some, was not so to us: but it was of short duration; when

morning came, we were again separated, and I never
saw her more. I remember the happiness of our
childish sports, the indulgence of maternal affection;
and fear that her lot would be still harder than mine,
fixed her image so indelibly on my mind, that neither
prosperity nor adversity has ever erased it.

"I once attempted to run away; but when I had
got into the woods, and night came on, I became
alarmed with the idea of being devoured by wild
beasts, and with trembling steps, and a sad heart, I
returned to my master's house, and laid down in his
fireplace, where I was found in the morning. Being
closely reprimanded by my master, he ordered me to
be taken care of, and I was soon sold again. I then
travelled through a very fertile country, where I saw
cocoa-nuts and sugar-cane.

"All the people I had hitherto seen, resembled my
own; and having learned a little of several languages,
I could understand them pretty well; but now, after
six or seven months had passed away, from the time
I was kidnapped, I arrived at the sea-coast, and I
beheld that element which before I had no idea of.
It also made me acquainted with such cruelties as I
can never reflect upon but with horror. The first
object that met my sight was a *slave ship* riding at
anchor, *waiting for her cargo !*

"When I was taken on board, being roughly
handled and closely examined by these men, whose
complexion and language differed so much from any
I had seen or heard before, I apprehended I had got

into a world of bad spirits, which so overcame me
that I fainted and fell.· When I came to, their horrible looks and red faces frightened me again exceedingly. But I had not time to think much about it,
before I was, with many of my poor country people,
put under deck in a loathsome and horrible place. In
this situation we wished for death, and sometimes
refused to eat, and for this we were beaten.

"After enduring more hardships than I can relate,
we arrived at Barbadoes, in the West Indies. When
taken on shore, we were put into a pen like so many
beasts, and thence sold and separated—husbands and
wives, parents and children, brothers and sisters,
without any distinction. Their cries excited some
compassion in the hearts of those who were capable
of feeling, but others seemed to feel no remorse,
though the scene was so affecting.

" I, with some others, was sent to America: when
we arrived in Virginia, we were also sold and separated. Not long after, Captain Pascal, coming to my
master's, purchased me, and sent me on board his
ship, called the Industrious Bee. I had not yet
learned much of the English language, so I could not
understand their conversation; and some of them
made me believe I was going home to Africa. This
pleased me very much, and the kind treatment I received made me happy ; but when we came in sight
of England, I found they had deceived me. It was
on board this ship I received the name of Gustavus
Vassa.

" Having often seen my master, and a lad named Richard Baker, who was very kind to me, reading in books, I had a desire to do so, that I might find out how all things had a beginning. For that purpose, I often took a book, talked to it, and then placed it to my ear to hear what it would say ; but when I found it remained silent, I was much concerned.

" The summer of 1757, I was taken by a press-gang, and carried on board a man-of-war. After passing about a year in this service, on the coast of France and in America, on my return to England, I received much kindness, and was sent to school, where I learned to read and write. My master receiving the office of lieutenant on board one of those ships, took me with him up the Mediterranean. My desire for learning induced some of my shipmates to instruct me, so that I could read the Bible ; and one of them, a sober man, explained many passages to me.

" As I had now served my master faithfully several years, and his kindness had given me hopes that he would grant my freedom when we arrived in England, I ventured to tell him so ; but he was offended, for he had determined on sending me to the West Indies. Accordingly, at the close of the year 1762, finding a vessel bound thither, he took me on board, and gave me in charge of the captain.

" I endeavored to expostulate with him, by telling him he had received my wages and all my prize money, but it was to no purpose. Taking my only coat from my back, he went off in his boat. I fol-

lowed them with aching eyes, and a heart ready to
burst with grief, until they were out of sight. The
captain, whose name was Doran, treated me very
kindly, but we had a tempestuous voyage.

" When we came in sight of Montserrat, remembering what I had seen on my first arrival from
Africa, it chilled me to the heart, and brought nothing to my view but misery, stripes, and chains : and
to complete my distress, two of the sailors robbed me
of about eight guineas, which I had collected by
doing little jobs on board the ships of war, and which
I hid when my master took my coat.

" Having unladed the ship, and laded her again
for sea, the captain sent for me : when, with trembling steps and a faltering heart, I came to him. I
found him sitting with Robert King, a Quaker,
and a merchant : and after telling me the charge he
had to get me a good master, he said he had got me
one of the best on the island. Mr. King also said
he had bought me on account of my good character (to
maintain which I found to be of great importance), and
that his home was in Philadelphia, where he expected
soon to go, and he did not intend to treat me hard.

" He asked me what I could do. I answered, I
can shave and dress hair pretty well; and that I have
learned to refine wines ; I could write, and understood arithmetic as far as the Rule of Three. The
character Captain Doran had given of my master, I
found to be correct. He possessed an amiable disposition, and was very charitable and humane.

" In passing about the island, I had an opportunity of seeing the dreadful usage, and wretched situation of the poor slaves; and it reconciled me to my
condition, and made me thankful for being placed
with so kind a master. He was several times offered a great price for me, but he would not sell me.
Having obtained three pence, I' began a little trade,
and soon gained a dollar, then more; with this I
bought me a Bible.

" Going in a vessel of my master's to Georgia and
Charleston, a small venture I took on my return
answered a very good purpose. In 1765, my master
prepared for going to Philadelphia. With his credit-
ing me for some articles, and the little stock of my
own, I laid in considerable, which elated me much ;
and I told him I hoped I should soon obtain enough
to purchase my freedom, which he promised me I
should have when I could pay him what he gave for
me.

" Between Montserrat and several ports in America
we made many trips. One circumstance occurred
when I was in Georgia that was a serious one to me.
Being in a yard with some slaves one evening, their
master coming home drunk, and seeing me, a stranger,
he, with a stout man to help him, beat me so that I
could not go aboard the ship, which gave the captain
much anxiety. When he found me, and saw the situation I was in, he wept; but by his kind attention,
and that of a skilful physician, I was in a few weeks
able to go on board and attend to my business.

" Thus, passing from one port to another, with my kind master's and captain's indulgence, and my own indefatigable industry and economy, I obtained the sum required for my liberty. So, one morning, while they were at breakfast, I ventured to remind my master of what he had promised, and to tell him I had got the money—at which he seemed surprised. The captain told him I had come honestly by it, and he must now fulfil his promise.

" Upon which he told me to get a manumission drawn, and he would sign it. At this intelligence my heart leaped for joy. When the whole was finished, and I was in reality free, I felt like another being—my joy was indescribable. My master and Captain Doran entreated me not to leave them, and gratitude induced me to stay, though I longed to see Captain Pascal, and let him know I was *free*.

" I now hired as a sailor, and our next voyage was to Savannah. When we were preparing to return, and were taking some cattle on board, one of them butted the captain in the breast, which affected him so that he was unable to do duty, and he died before we reached our port. This was a heavy stroke to me, for he had been my true friend, and I loved him as a father.

" The winter following, I sailed again for Georgia, with a new captain, in the Nancy : but steering a more westerly course than usual, we soon got on the Bahama banks, where our vessel was wrecked, but no lives were lost. Getting on one of the islands, with

some salt provision we had saved, we remained there
many days, and suffered much for want of fresh
water.

" When we were almost famished with hunger and
thirst, we were found and carried to New Providence,
where we were kindly treated. Thence we were taken
to Savannah, so to Martinico and Montserrat, having
been absent about six months, and experienced the
delivering hand of Providence more than once, when
all human means seemed hopeless.

" After relating to Mr. King the loss of the Nancy,
and the various hardships we had endured, I again
told him my desire to go to England ; and although
he wished me to remain in his service, he consented,
and gave me the following certificate :—' The bearer
hereof, Gustavus Vassa, was my slave upward of
three years; during which time he always behaved
himself well, and discharged his duty with honesty
and assiduity.—R. KING.'

" Obtaining this certificate, I soon parted with my
kind master, and arrived in England. When I here
received my wages, I had thirty-seven guineas. I
soon found my old captain, Pascal, who was surprised
to see me, and asked how I came back. I told him,
' In a ship.' To which he replied, ' I suppose you
did not *walk* on the *water*.'

" I now set my mind on getting more learning, and
attending school diligently. My money not being
sufficient, I hired myself to service a while ; but having a desire to go again to the Mediterranean, I

engaged on board a ship, where the mate taught me navigation. While at Smyrna, I saw many caravans from India. Among other articles, they brought great quantities of locusts, and a kind of pulse resembling French beans, though larger; they are sweet and palatable.

"In the spring of 1773, an expedition was fitted out to explore a northwest passage to India. Dr. Irving concluding to go, I accompanied him, and we went on board one of the vessels the 24th of May; and about the middle of June, by the use of the doctor's apparatus for making salt water fresh, we distilled from twenty-six to forty gallons a day. On the 28th we reached Greenland, where I found the sun did not set.

" We found large fields of ice, and to one of them, about eighty yards thick, we made our vessel fast: but we soon became so surrounded with ice that we could not move, and were in danger of being crushed to pieces. In this perilous situation we remained eleven days, when the weather becoming more mild, and the wind changing, the ice gave way, and in about thirty hours, with hard labor, we got into open water, to our great joy, and arrived at Deptford, after an absence of four months, wherein we had experienced imminent dangers.

" Rejoicing to be again in England, I entered into service, and remained a considerable time; during which I began to reflect seriously on the many dangers I had escaped, particularly in my last voyage, and it made a serious impression on my mind ; and my reflections were often turned to the awfulness of eternity.

" In this state, I took to my Bible, rejoicing that I could read it for myself, and I received encouragement. While my mind was thus seriously impressed, I went several voyages to Spain, and being often led to look over the occurrences of my past life, I saw there had been the hand of Providence to guide and protect me, though I knew it not ; and when I considered my obligations to the Lord for His goodness, I wept.

" On our return, the last voyage, we picked up eleven Portuguese. Their vessel had sunk, with two of the crew, and they were in a small open boat, without victuals, compass, water, or anything else, and must soon have perished. As soon as they got on board our vessel, they fell on their knees and thanked God for their deliverance. Thus I saw verified what was written in the 107th Psalm.

" From the year 1777 to 1784, I remained more quiet ; but about the latter period I made a trip to New York, and one to Philadelphia. At the latter place, I was very much pleased to see the worthy Quakers easing the burdens of my oppressed countrymen. It also rejoiced my heart when one of these people took me to the free school, and I saw the children of my color instructed, and their minds cultivated to fit them for usefulness. -

" Not long after my return, I found government

was preparing to make a settlement of free people of color on the coast of Africa, and that vessels were engaged to carry such as wished to go to Sierra Leone. I engaged as commissary, and we set sail with 426 persons. But the time of our arrival there, the rainy season having commenced, proved unfavorable, and some of us soon returned to England; where, since that period, I have been doing what I could for the relief of my much-injured country people.

"Having been early taught to look for the hand of God in minute circumstances, they have been of consequence to me; and aiming at simple truth in relating the incidents of my life, I hope some of my readers will gather instruction from them."

Gregorie, in his Inquiry into the Intellectual and Moral Faculties of the Negroes, states, that after thirty years of a wandering and stormy life, Vassa established himself in London, where he married, and published his memoirs, which have been several times reprinted—the last edition in 1794; and it is proved by the most respectable testimony that he was the author. In 1789, he presented a petition to parliament for the suppression of the slave trade.

He also says, that a son of his, named Sancho, having received a good education, was an assistant librarian to Sir Joseph Banks, and secretary to the committee for vaccination. And he concludes with this remark: "If Vassa still lived, the bill which was lately passed, prohibiting the slave trade, would be consoling to his heart, and to his old-age."

BILLY AND JENNY.

About the year 1738, a man and his wife, named Tom and Caty, who were in bondage to Thomas Bowne, on Long Island, had a little son whom they called Billy. This little boy, when old enough to work, was sold to a farmer in the neighborhood; who, according to the custom of those days, went with his servants into the field, and allotted to each one his portion of labor. By this means, Billy became acquainted with the different branches of husbandry, and was inured to industry.

With this farmer, he was pretty comfortably cared for, and kept to his daily labor until the thirty-first year of his age. About the year 1744, the master of one of those ships employed in bringing the poor Africans from their native land, among others brought away a little girl—too young, alas! to tell even by what means, or in what way she was taken.

This little girl, after suffering all the hardships attendant on her situation, and a long confinement on shipboard, was landed in New York, and sold according to the custom of that time. She was bought by Samuel Underhill, and taken to Long Island to wait on his wife and children and they called her Jenny. As she advanced in age, she became more and more useful in her master's family, and satisfied with her situation.

Her mistress being a woman of an uncommonly amiable disposition, having known the subjugation of her own will, by the operation of that principle which brings into harmony all the discordant passions, and one of that description also, that " looked well to the ways of her household, and ate not the bread of idleness," she was qualified to govern her family with mildness and discretion, and to set them an example of economy, sobriety, cheerfulness, and industry.

Jenny, being placed under the tuition of such a mistress, in due time became qualified to fill the station allotted her with propriety, as an honest, sober, industrious, and useful servant. When she had arrived at about the twentieth year of her age, she was visited by the before-mentioned Billy, in the character of a suitor. After mature deliberation, and their affections becoming more strongly fixed, with the approbation of those concerned, the marriage ceremony was performed.

Thus were they united, not only in the bonds of wedlock, but those of sincere affection, which abundantly manifested itself in their conduct toward and respect for each other, during a long and laborious life, and in their care of their numerous offspring, which consisted of nine sons and one daughter.

Time passing on with them, they partook of such a share of happiness as their situation in life would permit, until the year 1769, when the master of Jenny, having purchased a farm in Westchester county, was preparing to remove his family thither. This circumstance became a very close trial to this affectionate pair, who by this time had several children.

The thoughtfulness and anxiety felt by them on this occasion being reciprocated by their masters, a proposition was made for an exchange. The wife of one of Billy's fellow-servants being in the family with Jenny, accommodations were soon made, and Billy was admitted a resident in the family with his beloved partner : when they all proceeded to their new settlement, where they lived in harmony and concord for many years, and until their master's children were all married and settled.

During this period, Billy and Jenny, with all their children, were liberated by their master, and such of them as were old enough, were placed, where they might be brought up to habits of industry, and be prepared to provide for themselves a comfortable subsistence ; but Billy and Jenny remained with him.

Age and infirmity at length put a period to their kind master's life. And his family, being thus deprived of his care and exertions, were induced to leave their abode. The mistress, who had long exercised an affectionate care over her household, finding herself lonely, retired to live with her children. And with her youngest son, she remained to an advanced age, and was then gathered into rest, as a shock of corn in its season.

Billy and Jenny having a house provided for them, remained under the care of their former master's descendants, and with their own industry, and the generosity of their friends, they were comfortably situated. But when Billy was so disabled by infirm-

ity, that he could not work as a day-laborer, he cultivated a little garden, and did some light jobs for his
neighbors.

Their children being out, while Jenny's health and
strength remained, she went out to washing and house-
cleaning. Billy generally waited on her to the place
of destination, and then, returning to his habitation,
nursed his garden, and poultry until toward evening,
when he would go to accompany her home. More
genuine politeness and unremitting attention, between a man and his wife, are rarely to be found, in
city or country, than were manifested by this sable
pair.

Thus they lived several years; but Jenny at length
became enfeebled by age, and her sight failed, so that
she was no longer capable of laboring abroad, or using
her spinning-wheel at home, as heretofore, which
made it necessary for them to be placed in a different
situation. One winter, while they remained at house-
keeping, there came a very severe snow-storm, with
high wind, so that passing from one place to another
was rendered very difficult for several days.

As soon as practicable, their friend, who had the
care of them, and supplied their wants, went to see
how they fared; when Jenny, meeting him at the
door, and being asked how they were, etc., said, " Oh,
Master Richard, I am wonderful glad to see thee—if
the storm had lasted much longer, I believe we
should have froze to death; our wood was 'most
gone, and Billy is one of the honestest niggers in the

world ; for he had rather freeze to death than steal a
rail from the fence." This circumstance is recorded
as one specimen of their honest simplicity.

In the spring of 1815, they were removed to the
habitation of one of their sons, where they were
boarded ; and there they remained, until death, the
destroyer of all earthly comforts, put a period to
Jenny's life, after a few days' severe illness, about the
seventy-eighth year of her age.

The same affectionate attachment that pervaded
her mind in youth and in health, remained unshaken
to the last. Her sight, as before remarked, being
almost gone, when lying on her bed, she frequently
inquired for Billy; but when she was told he was
lying behind her, or sitting by her, she was satisfied.

Thus she closed a long and laborious life, beloved
and respected for her many good qualities, and her
consistent conduct. Billy died at Scarsdale, Westchester county, New York, on the 4th of Third month,
1826, after a few days' illness, aged about eighty-seven
years, and was decently interred by the side of Jenny,
on the 6th of the same month.

GEORGE HARDY.

DURING the winter of 1832, the writer of the narrative of which this account is an abridgment, became
acquainted with Hannah Hardy, an interesting old

colored woman, and her son George. They were the
suffering tenants of a miserable garret, lighted only
by a few panes of glass, and ill-secured from the in-
clemencies of the weather.

Hannah had been an industrious woman, who supported herself comfortably for many years, until her
sight, which had long been declining, so nearly left
her as to disqualify her for all kinds of work. George,
who was her youngest son, disclosed in his earliest
years great quickness of discernment and readiness of
apprehension. He could read the Bible when only
four years old; and he continued to be remarkable
for docility, and for preferring his books and other
profitable employments to the idle sports of children.

When about eleven years old, he was placed from
home, where he remained until four years since, when
he became so much diseased with scrofula as to make
it necessary for him to return to his mother. From
that time, she became his constant and only nurse,
and evinced, through numberless privations and difficulties, the most unwearied attention and patient en-
durance.

When he was able to sit up and use his arms, he
made rope-mats; by which, with casual help from his
friends, he supported his mother and paid her rent.
He always mended his own and her clothes, and
allowed no time to pass away in idleness, which he
was able to employ; and so cheerful, so thankful, and
so happy did this interesting couple appear, that it
afforded a lesson of instruction to be with them.

Hannah, who could only distinguish the glare of
noon from the gloom of darkness, had lived so long
in the forlorn tenement they then inhabited, and
knew so well all the turnings of its steep and dangerous stairs, that she could not bear to hear the proposal from some of her friends to provide one more
comfortable.   Through the latter part of the winter,
and the commencement of the spring, George's sufferings greatly increased ; he was wholly confined to his
bed, and so emaciated with pain and disease, that
although he was seventeen years of age, his arms were
not thicker than an infant's.

He had been a diligent reader of the Holy Scriptures ; and though he told me they had been to
him a sealed book, until he was brought to that bed
of suffering, yet it was evident that his mind had long
been enabled to appropriate to his own necessities
many of their precious precepts.   Though he labored
under the combined effects of scrofula and dropsy, in
their highest degrees of virulence, yet I never heard
him repine ; and often, while suffering extreme bodily
anguish, he would speak of the relief it afforded the
poor afflicted body, to have the mind composed and
tranquil, and would say, " O, I feel like a poor worm
in the fire ; yet all I desire is, to be favored with
patience to bear all my pain, and with a willing mind
to wait the Master's will to take me away."

For many days and nights together he was able to
obtain but little sleep ; yet he showed no marks of
restlessness or discontent.   Once, calling me to his

bedside, he said, "I am afraid I am not patient enough ; but I often feel very weary, and I fear I shall wear my poor mother out. I am more · concerned for her than for myself—what should I do for a care-taker if she were gone ? She is very kind to me, and I have many kind friends. I am afraid I am not grateful enough for all my favors. To some, this garret would look like a dull place, but it never looks gloomy to me ; I have had more pleasure in it than I could have had in the nicest parlor."

Having called one day after he had passed a sleepless and languishing night, I found him, with the Bible fixed before him, reading. He looked animated, and said, " I always loved to read the Bible, but I never understood it until very lately ; now I understand it, and I find that religion and pleasure are in no way inconsistent. I feel now that I shall never recover. I am willing to die, and I shall be happy when I am gone from earth—but the Lord is very merciful, and can make me happy as long as He chooses that I should stay. I have trusted in Him through pain and through want, and I believe He will never forsake me. My Fifth has sometimes been closely tried, but I never let go my confidence."

His disease now rapidly increased, and with it his suffering. On the 23d of Fifth month, he conversed a long time with the doctor, and seemed more comfortable than usual ; but he passed a sleepless and distressing night. The next day, he was able to take but little nourishment, owing to the great soreness of his mouth and throat, but he could converse intelligibly, and seemed anxious to do so. About two o'clock this day, I found him in great pain, but quite tranquil in mind.

On my going to him, he said, " My sufferings are now nearly over; I shall not live many days—not more than two. The Lord's time has nearly come, and then He will take me where I shall never suffer any more. O, how marvellous His mercy is, to look down upon such a polluted sinner as I am !

'1 the worst of sinners am,
But Jesus came to save me.'—

Yes, He will save me—I know it. I have a hope—a pretty certain hope—O, it is a very certain hope—it is a very sure hope." He then in a low and indistinct voice, supplicated for many minutes; after which he said, " I have been talking to my Saviour."

Not expecting him to hear, I asked his mother if he had always been a serious boy; but before she could reply, George said, " No ! I was always bad, always wicked ; but since I was brought to this bed of sickness, I have sought for repentance, and I have found it: my sins were as scarlet, but now they are washed as white as snow. But it is all mercy, pure mercy; we have no righteousness of our own to depend upon—no works, no merit of our own will avail us at such a time as this. If these were all we had to look to, we should never be saved. But this

is what Jesus came into the world for—to save us
poor sinners ; and salvation belongs to Him alone."

After this, he desired me to read to him in the
Bible—said he would like to hear me read in the
Psalms, where David deplored his sins. I did so,
and he afterward composed himself and slept a few
minutes ; but the pain soon awoke him, and he said,
" I hope my patience will hold out—I must not get
impatient so near the end."

On the 25th, his sufferings greatly increased, and
on the afternoon of the 26th, he was unable longer to
speak, but he appeared to be sensible of what was
passing, and to know those about him. He several
times embraced his mother very tenderly and wept.
The impress which the pain and anguish of the pre-
ceding day had left upon his countenance, now yielded
to a placid and heavenly serenity ; and his breath
continued to shorten, until he ceased to breathe.

LOTT CAREY.

PRINCIPALLY FROM GURLEY'S LIFE OF ASHMUN.

This interesting individual was born a slave, on
the estate of William A. Christian, in Charles City
county, about thirty miles below Richmond.   In
1804, he was sent to that city, and hired out by the
year as a common laborer at the Shockoe warehouse.

At that time, and for two or three years after, he was excessively profane, and much addicted to intoxication.

But God, who is rich in mercy, was pleased to awaken him to a sense of his lost estate; and in the year 1807, he made open profession of his faith in the Saviour. A sermon which he heard about that time, founded on our Lord's interview with Nicodemus, awakened in him so strong a desire to be able to read and write, that he obtained a Testament, and commenced learning his letters, by trying to read the chapter in which that interview is recorded.

He was occasionally instructed by young gentlemen at the warehouse, though he never attended a regular school. In a little time, he was able to read and write, so as to make dray tickets, and superintend the shipping of tobacco. In this business, and in overseeing the labor of the other hands in the warehouse, he was particularly useful; so much so, that he received 800 dollars salary in 1820, the last year he remained there; and he could have received a larger sum, if he would have continued.

In the year 1813, he bought himself and his two little children (his wife being dead) for 850 dollars, and thus became free. The manner in which he obtained this sum of money to purchase himself and his children, reflects much credit on his character. It will be seen from the salary he received after he was free, and which he relinquished for the sake of doing good in Africa, that his services at the warehouse were highly estimated; but of their real value, no one except a dealer in tobacco can form an idea. Notwithstanding the hundreds of hogsheads that were committed to his charge, he could produce any one the instant it was called for; and the shipments were made with a promptness and correctness, such as no person has equalled in the same situation. For this correctness and fidelity, he was highly esteemed, and frequently rewarded by the merchant with a five-dollar note. He was allowed also to sell for his benefit many small parcels of waste tobacco. It was by saving the little sums obtained in this way, with the aid of a subscription by the merchants to whose interests he had been attentive, that he procured these 850 dollars which he paid for the freedom of himself and children. When the colonists were fitted out for Africa, he defrayed a considerable part of his own expense. With a design to improve his condition, he emigrated to Africa among the first settlers of Liberia, where he was the means of doing much good to both colonists and natives.

In reply to one of his friends, who desired to know what inducement he had for going to Africa, when he was already so comfortably situated, he said, " I am an African; and in this country, however meritorious my conduct and respectable my character, I cannot receive the credit due to either. I wish to go to a country where I shall be estimated by my merits, not by my complexion. And I likewise feel bound to labor for my suffering race."

9

Soon after he made a profession of religion he commenced holding meetings and exhorting among the
colored people; and, though he had scarcely any
knowledge of books, and but little acquaintance with
mankind, he would frequently exhibit a boldness of
thought, and a strength of native intellect, which no
acquirement could ever have given him.

At the close of his farewell sermon, on his departure for Africa, he remarked in substance as follows:
" I am about to leave you; and I expect to see your
faces no more.   I long to preach to the poor Africans
the way of life and salvation.   I don't know what
may befall me—whether I may find a grave in the
ocean, or among the savage men, or more savage wild
beasts, on the coast of Africa : nor am I anxious what
may become of me; I feel it my duty to go.

" I very much fear that many of those who preach
the gospel in this country will blush when the
Saviour calls them to give an account of their labors
in His cause, and tells them, ' I commanded you to go
into all the world, and preach the gospel to every
creature.' "   And with the most forcible emphasis he
exclaimed, " The Saviour may ask, ' Where have you
been ?   What have you been doing?   Have you
endeavored to the utmost of your ability to fulfil the
commands I gave you ? or have you sought your own
gratification and your own ease, regardless of my commands ? ' "

In his new home, his intellectual ability, firmness
of purpose, unbending integrity, correct judgment,

and disinterested benevolence, caused him ' to be beloved and respected, and gave him great influence : and he soon rose to honorable distinction. The interests of the colony, and the cause of his countrymen, in both Africa and America, were very near to his heart. For them he was willing to toil, and to make almost any sacrifice ; and he frequently declared that no possessions in America could induce him to return.

He possessed. a constitution peculiarily fitted for toil and exposure, and he felt the effects of the climate perhaps less than any other individual in the colony. During the sickly season of the year, he was usually wholly employed in attending the sick ; and for more than a year, they had no other physician among them. The little medical information he had obtained from Dr. Ayres and others on the coast, together with several years' experience, enabled him successfully to contend with the peculiar fevers of the climate.

Under date of March 12th, 1824, shortly after the arrival of the Cyrus with 105 emigrants, he wrote : " The fever began about the 24th ult., and on the 28th we had thirty-eight cases; and by the 2d inst. we had sixty-six under the operation of medicine; and at present, I have about a hundred cases of fever to contend with ; but we have been very much favored, for they all appear to be on the recovery, and we have lost none, saving three children. I have very little time to write to you, myself being the only man that will venture to act in the capacity of a physician."

The managers of the American Colonization Society, in 1825, invited Carey to visit the United States, in the expectation that his intelligent and candid statements, concerning the condition and prospects of the colony and the moral wants of Africa, would exert a beneficial influence on the opinions of the people of color, and recommend the cause of the society to the public regard.

In the month of April, 1826, he made arrangements to embark in the Indian Chief, on her return from taking a large number of emigrants to the colony, and received from Ashmun testimonials of his worth and services. The following is an extract from a letter from Ashmun to the managers of the Colonization Society :

" The Rev. Lott Carey has, in my opinion, some claims on the justice of the society, or the government of the United States, or both, which merit consideration. These claims arise out of a long and faithful course of medical services rendered to this colony. More than one-half of his time has been given up to the care of the sick, from the day I landed in Africa to the very moment of stating the fact. He has personally aided, in every way that fidelity and benevolence could dictate, in all the attentions which our sick have in so long a period received.

" Several times have these disinterested labors reduced him to the very verge of the grave. He has

hitherto received no compensation, either from the
society or the government, for these services. I need
not add, that it has not been in his power to support
himself and family, by any use he could make of the
remnants of the time left him, after discharging the
amount of duties devolving upon him. In addition,
he has the care of the liberated Africans."

Until near the time of the Indian Chief's departure,
he cherished the hope of embarking in her for America. But as there was no other physician in the
colony, it was finally thought best for him to postpone
his departure until another opportunity.

Notwithstanding he on one occasion manifested a
disposition for insubordination, yet, like a wise man
and a Christian, he soon saw his error, and acknow-
ledged it with humility and submission. He was
elected in September, 1826, to the vice-agency of the
colony, and discharged the duties of that important
office until his death.

In his good sense, moral worth, public spirit, courage, resolution, and decision, the colonial agent had
perfect confidence. He knew that in times of difficulty or of danger, full reliance might be placed upon
the energy and efficiency of Carey.

When compelled, in the early part of 1828, to
leave the colony, Ashmun committed the administra-
tion of the colonial affairs into the hands of the vice-
agent, in the full belief that no interest would be betrayed, but that his efforts would be constantly and
anxiously directed to the promotion of the public good.

Soon after Carey wrote thus : " Feeling very sensibly my incompetency to enter upon the duties of my office, without first making all the officers of the colony well acquainted with the principal objects which should engage our attention, I invited them to meet at the Agency House on the 27th, at nine o'clock, which was punctually attended to, and I then read all the instructions left by Mr. Ashman, without reserve, and requested their co-operation. To get the new settlers located on their lands, was a very important item in my instructions ; and I trust, through the blessing of the great Ruler of events, we shall be able to realize all the expectations of Mr. Ashmun."

He soon purchased a large tract of land for the Colonization Society of the native kings ; and further said, " Captain Russell will be able to give something like a fair account of the state of our improvements, as he went with me to visit the settlements, and seemed pleased with the prospect at Millsburg, Caldwell, and the Halfway Farms."

For about six months after the departure of Ashmun from the colony, Carey stood at its head, and conducted himself with such energy and wisdom as to do honor to his previous reputation, and fix the seal upon his enviable fame. But, alas ! he was suddenly and unexpectedly, and in a distressing manner, forced from life, in all its vigor, by the explosion of gunpowder, on the 8th of November, in which eight persons lost their lives.

Carey was thrice married, and thrice he was left a widower. His first wife died, as before related, previous to his becoming free. His second wife died at Foura Bay, near Sierra Leone, shortly after arriving in Africa. Of her triumphant death, he has given a most affecting account in his journal of that date. His third wife died at Cape Montserado. She was the daughter of Richard Sampson, from Petersburg.

It has been very well said of Carey, that he was one of nature's noblemen. Had he possessed the advantages of education, few men of his age would have excelled him in knowledge or genius. To found a Christian colony which might prove a blessed asylum to his degraded brethren in America, and enlighten and regenerate Africa, was, in his view, an object with which no temporal good, not even life, could be compared.

The strongest sympathies of his nature were excited in behalf of his unfortunate people, and the divine promise cheered and encouraged him in his labors for their improvement and salvation. A main pillar in the society and church of Liberia has fallen! But we will not despond. The memorial of his worth shall never perish. It shall stand in a clearer light, when every chain is broken, and Christianity shall have assumed her sway over the millions of Africa.

THE GOOD MASTER AND HIS FAITHFUL SLAVE.

Translated from the French.

WARNER MIFFLIN, for his candor, affability, and knowledge, was ranked among those who are an honor to their country and their age. He had received from his father thirty-seven negroes, old and young. The day that he had fixed upon for their emancipation being come, he called one after another into his chamber, and this was the conversation that passed with one of them :

"Well, my friend James, how old art thou ? "   "I am twenty-nine and a half years old, master." "Thou shouldst have been free, as thy white brethren are, at twenty-one.   Religion and humanity enjoin me this day to give thee thy liberty, and justice requires me to pay thee for eight and a half years' service, at the rate of twenty-one pounds and five shillings per annum, including in it thy food and raiment, making altogether a sum of ninety-five pounds, twelve shillings, and sixpence owing to thee; but as thou art young and healthy, thou hadst better work for thy living : my intention is to give thee a bond for it, bearing interest at the rate of seven per cent.

" Thou hast now no master but God and the laws. Go into the next room ; thou wilt find there thy late mistress and my nephew ; they are engaged in writing thy manumission. May God bless thee, James! Be wise and industrious; in all thy trials, thou wilt find a friend in thy old master."

James, surprised at a scene so new and affecting, shed many tears; astonishment, gratitude, and a variety of feelings, shook his frame. He shed a flood of tears, and could scarcely articulate these words: "Ah, my master! why do you give me my liberty? I have always had what I wanted: we have worked together in the fields, and I have worked as much for myself as for you.

"I have eaten of the same food, and been clothed like you—and we have gone together on foot to meeting. We have the Sabbath to ourselves: we don't lack any thing. When we are sick, our good and tender mistress comes to our bedside, always saying something consolatory to us. Ah, my dear master! when I am free, where shall I go? and when I am sick—"

"Thou shalt be as the whites; thou shalt hire with those who will give thee generous wages: in a few years, thou shalt purchase a piece of land, marry a wife, wise and industrious as thyself, and rear up children, as I have reared thee, in the fear of the Lord and love of labor. After having lived free and happy, thou shalt die in peace.

"Thou *must* accept liberty, James; it is a great while since it was due to thee. Would to God, the Father of all men, that the whites had never thought of trading in thy African brethren; may He inspire all men with the desire of following our example.

9*

We, who regard liberty as the first of blessings, why should we refuse it to those who live among us ? "

"Ah, my master ! you are so good is the reason I wish not to leave you—*I have never been a slave.* You have never spoken to me but as you speak to white men ; I have lacked nothing, either in sickness or in health ; I have never worked more than your neighbors, who have worked for themselves.

" I have been richer than many whites—to some of whom I have lent money. And my good and tender mistress never commands us to do anything, but makes us do everything by only saying, ' Please to do it.' How shall 1 leave you ? give me by the year what you will, in the name of a freeman or a slave, it is of little consequence to me—I shall never be happy but with you—I will never leave you."

" Well, James, I consent to what thou desirest ; after thy manumission shall have passed through the necessary forms, I will hire thee by the year ; but take at least one of relaxation ; it is a great epoch of thy life ; celebrate it with joy, and rest by doing whatsoever thou wilt."

" No master ! it is seed time—I will take my pleasure another time—one day only shall be a holiday in my family. •Then, since you will have it so, I will accept my liberty ; and my first action, as a free man, is to take your hand, my master, press it between mine, and lay it on my heart, where the attachment and gratitude of James will not cease until that ceases 'to beat ; and until that moment be assured that no laborer in the county of Kent will be more industrious than he who henceforth shall be called FAITHFUL JAMES."

EZEKIEL COSTON,

AGED upwards of eighty-three years, related to Samuel Canby, of Wilmington, Delaware, in 1825, the following circumstances of his freedom from his master, the late Warner Mifflin, a Quaker: and it may be observed, that he always supported an unblemished character:

That he was born a slave in the family of Daniel Mifflin, of Accomack county, Virginia, with whom he lived until about twenty years of age; about which period Warner Mifflin (son of Daniel) married a daughter of John Kensey's, of West River, Maryland, and settled near Camden, in the State of Delaware. Ezekiel, and five other slaves, were given him by his father; there were also a number of slaves belonging to his wife brought into the family.

He lived with Warner Mifflin about eighteen months, when he put him on a plantation of his to work it, about six miles from his residence, where he continued about four years a slave. At this period Ezekiel was informed by his master that he had concluded to set his slaves free; and very soon after his master came to his residence, and calling him from the field

where he was ploughing, they sat down together, when
he told Ezekiel his mind had long been uneasy with
holding slaves, and that he must let him go.

Ezekiel was so well satisfied with his present situation, that he told his master he could not leave him.
Their conversation on the subject produced such feelings of tenderness that they *both wept much.* Finally,
as an inducement to comply, his master told him he
might remain on the farm, and they entered into a
mutual engagement, which was carried into effect, and
Ezekiel continued to live on the farm fourteen years,
when his master gave him a piece of land, upon which
he built a house, where he remained until he came into
the neighborhood of Wilmington, where and in that
town he has resided until the present time.

After relating the foregoing narrative, he was inquired of respecting the account entitled " The Good
Master and his Faithful Slave "—a circumstance
which took place about the time of his being liberated, and in the same family—to which he bore the
following testimony, shedding many tears while the
reader was pursuing the theme, saying, " It is just so,
poor Jem and I lived together with master, and
worked together in harmony. How well I remember
when Jem told me that Master Mifflin had done the
same by him as he had done for me.

" It is all true—mistress brought a number of
slaves with her into the family, after master married
her—one of them was my wife—all the rest of us,
making, I suppose about thirty, were given by old

master to Master Warner, who is now an angel in heaven. Oh, how it comforts me to believe that, after suffering a few more pains, I shall live with him for ever in communion sweet! We were brought up children together, slept together, eat at the same table, and never quarrelled."

The dear old man seems indeed like one waiting with Christian resignation for an entrance into the heavenly kingdom. I have no doubt of the correctness of his testimony. He appears to have as perfect a recollection of the days of his childhood as though they had just passed.

AN ANECDOTE,

Communicated to a Friend on the way from Charleston to Savannah by a Fellow-Passenger.

A SLAVE belonging to his grandmother was carried off when a boy by the British, in the time of the revolutionary war, to Nova Scotia, where he lived several years; but he did not forget his old home and friends, and he returned to his mistress, giving himself up as a slave. But she, not having employment for him, talked of selling him. He told her if she did, he was determined to destroy himself, for that it was nothing but his attachment to the family that brought him back. He was then suffered to work out, paying a certain part of his wages to his owner.

The family soon after became embarrassed ; and one of the grandsons was sent to the West Indies to a relation. Just as he was embarking, the faithful black put into his hand a purse containing all his little earnings, and insisted upon his young master's taking it, saying he had no use for the money himself, and his master might want it in a strange country, away from his friends. The slave, still living in Charleston, was suffered to work for himself. He has had repeated offers of his liberty, but he prefers living in the family that brought him up. '

THE COLORED FOUNDLING.

A POOR, but honest and respectable old man, whose name was Hector, resided in Philadelphia. He and his wife lived on the scanty earnings of their own hands, in a very small cottage. One evening, at a late hour, a woman of their own color, with an infant, stopped at their dwelling and asked for a night's lodging, to which his wife answered, " We can't lodge you, we got but one bed." " Oh," said the old man, seeing her a stranger and in difficulty, " let her tag [stay], she sleep in de bed with you, I go make a bed on de floor—must not turn her out o' doors."

The woman accordingly stayed; and in the night, Hector was awakened by the cries of the child. He arose to ascertain the cause of it, and found the mother was gone; on which he aroused his wife, saying,

" Well, Sukey, you see de woman has gone off and lef' de child for you." " Oh," said his wife, "what shall we do now ? She never come again." " Well," returned Hector, " then you must take care of him: who knows God Almighty send him here for something—may be to take care of us in our old age—must not turn him out o' doors."

So they fed and nourished it with milk from the market—the old man going regularly to procure it. No one appearing, the child became their adopted. When he had attained the age of eight or nine years, proving an active lad, they put him to a chimney sweeper, as the most likely way for him to become early useful, and he soon contributed a little to his guardian's subsistence.

They at length grow quite infirm, and the wife died. After which, the neighbors, thinking it too much for the lad to have the whole care of the old man, prevailed on him to go to the Bettering House. When there the boy did not forsake but frequently visited him, and continued to add to his support until he died ; a few days after which the lad died also, having grown up beloved and respected.

THE GRATEFUL NEGRO.

SOME years since, a gentleman, who was the possessor of considerable property, from various causes became embarrassed in his circumstances and was arrested by his creditors, and confined in the king's bench prison; whence there was no probability of his being liberated, unless some law proceedings (upon his succeeding in which the recovery of a great part of his property depended) were decided in his favor.

Thus situated, he called a colored man who had for many years served him with the greatest faithfulness, and said, "Robert, you have lived with me many years, but I am now unable to maintain you any longer; you must leave me, and endeavor to find another master."

The poor man, well remembering his master's kindness, replied, "No, massa, me no leave you; you maintain me many years, me now try what I can do for you." Robert then went and procured employment as a day laborer, and regularly brought his earnings to his master; on which, though small, they managed to subsist for some time, until the law-suit was decided in the master's favor, and he thereby regained possession of a very considerable property.

Mindful of his faithful servant, one of his first acts was to settle an annuity upon him for the remainder of his life, sufficient to secure to the poor fellow the enjoyment of those comforts he had so well deserved.

This little anecdote may afford instruction both to the nominal and professing Christian : let the former inquire, Should I have acted thus, if in a similar situation?

THE FAITHFUL NURSE.

FROM THE LADIES' MONTHLY MUSEUM.

In the dreadful earthquake which made such ravages in the island of St. Domingo, in the year 1770, a colored nurse found herself alone in the house of her master and mistress, with the youngest child, which she nursed. The house shook to its foundation. Every one had taken flight; she alone could not escape, without leaving her infant charge in danger.

She flew to the chamber, where it lay in the most profound sleep. At the moment the walls of the house fell in, anxious only for the safety of her foster child, she threw herself over it, and serving as a sort of arch, saved it from destruction. The child was indeed saved; but the unfortunate nurse died soon after, the victim of her fidelity.

COFFIN.

FROM DR. MOYES'S LECTURES.

DURING the late war a gentleman and his wife were going from the East Indies to England. His wife died on the passage, and left two infants, the charge of which fell to a colored boy about seventeen years of age. The gentleman, for some reason which I do not recollect, went on board the vessel of the commodore of the fleet in which they sailed. There came on a violent storm, and the vessel which the children were on board of was on the point of being lost.

They despatched a boat from the commodore's vessel, to save as many as they could. They had almost filled the boat, and there was room enough for the infants, or the negro boy. What did he do? He did not hesitate a moment, but put the children into the boat, and said, " Tell my master that Coffin has done his duty ; " and that instant he was received into the bosom of the ocean, never more to return. The queen requested the celebrated poetess, Hannah Moore, to write an epic poem on it, but she wisely declined it, saying that no art could embellish so noble a sentiment.

JAMES DERHAM,

ORIGINALLY a slave in Philadelphia, was sold by his master to a physician, who employed him in his shop as assistant in the preparation of drugs. During the war between America and England he was sold to a surgeon, and by that surgeon to Dr. Robert Dove, of New Orleans. He learned the English, French, and Spanish languages, so as to speak them with ease.

He was received a member of the English church; and in the year 1788, when he was about twenty-one years of age, he became one of the most distinguished physicians in New Orleans. "I conversed with him on medicine," says Dr. Rush, and " found him very learned. I thought I could give *him* information concerning the treatment of diseases, but I learned more from him than he could expect from me."

The Pennsylvania Society, established in favor of the people of color, thought it their duty, in 1789, to publish these facts, which are also related by Dickson, page 184. In the Domestic Medicine of Buchan, and in a work of Duplaint, we find accounts of a cure for the bite of the rattlesnake. I know not whether Derham was its discoverer, but it is a well-known fact that one of his color did make such a discovery, for which he received, from the General Assembly of Carolina, his freedom and an annuity of a hundred pounds sterling.

THE AFRICAN PRINCE.

In the most flourishing period of the reign of Louis XIV. two African youths, the sons of a prince, being brought to the court of France, the king appointed a Jesuit to instruct them in letters and in the Christian religion; and gave to each of them a commission in his guards. The elder, who was remarkable for candor and ingenuousness, made great improvement, more particularly in the doctrines of religion.

A brutal officer, upon some dispute, insulted him with a blow. The gallant youth never so much as offered to resent it. A person who was his friend took an opportunity to talk with him that evening alone upon his behavior, which he told him was too tame, especially in a soldier. "Is there then," said the young African, "one revelation for soldiers, and another for merchants and gownsmen? The good father to whom I owe all my knowledge, has earnestly inculcated in me forgiveness of injuries; assuring me that a Christian was by no means to retaliate abuses of any kind."

"The good father," replied his friend, "may fit you for a monastery, by his lessons, but never for the army and the rules of a court. In a word," continued he, "if you do not call the colonel to an account, you will be branded with the infamy of cowardice, and have your commission taken from you." "I would fain," said the young man, "act consistently in every thing; but since you press me with that regard to my honor which you have always shown, I will wipe off so foul a stain; though I must own I gloried in it before."

Immediately upon this, he desired his friend to go from him and appoint the aggressor to meet him early in the morning. Accordingly, they met and fought, and the brave African youth disarmed his adversary, and forced him to ask his pardon publicly. This done, the next day he threw up his commission, and desired the king's leave to return to his father.

At parting, he embraced his brother and his friends, with tears in his eyes, saying that he had not imagined Christians to be so unaccountable a people; that he could not apprehend their faith could be of any use to them, if it did not influence their practice; and that, in his country, they thought it no dishonor to act according to the principles of their religion.

UNCLE HARRY.

FROM THE LITERARY AND EVANGELICAL MAGAZINE,
1824.

LATE in the last autumn it was my privilege (says the author) to spend a few hours in the hospitable mansion of the Rev. S. B. W., of F. I arrived at his house very early in the morning, just before the family assembled to perform their customary devo-

tions. On the signal being given, the children and
domestics came into the room where we were sitting.

Among the latter, there was a very aged colored
man, whom every one called Uncle Harry. As soon
as he entered, I observed that Mr. W. and his lady
treated him with marked attention and kindness.
The morning was sharp and frosty, and Uncle Harry
had a chair in the corner, close to the fire.

The portion of Scripture selected for the service
was the second chapter of Luke. I observed that the
attention of Harry was deeply fixed, and he soon began to manifest strong emotions. The old man's eye
kindled as the reader went on, and when he came to
the tenth verse, Harry appeared as though his heart
was tuned to the angelic song, and he could hardly
help uttering a shout of triumph.

There was not, however, the smallest ostentation
of feeling, or endeavor to attract attention. He only,
in a gentle manner, turned his face upward, strongly
clasping his hands as they lay on his lap, and express-
ing by his countenance the joy of his heart. By this
time he had interested me so highly that I could not
keep my eyes from him.

I watched the varying expressions of his countenance, and saw that every word seemed to strike on
his heart, and produce a corresponding emotion. I
thought I would give the world, if I could *read* the
Bible just as Harry *heard* it. While I was thinking,
and looking on with intense interest, the reader came
to the passage where old Simeon saw the infant

Saviour, took him in his arms, blessed God, and said.
" Lord, now lettest thou thy servant depart in peace,
for mine eyes have seen thy salvation."

Harry's emotion had become stronger and stronger,
until the words just quoted were read, when he was
completely overpowered. Suddenly turning on his
seat, to hide as much as possible his feelings, he bent
forward and burst into a flood of tears; but they
were tears of joy. He anticipated his speedy peaceful departure and his final rest. This state of feeling
continued during the remainder of the service, and
when we rose from our knees, Uncle Harry's face
seemed literally to have been bathed in tears.

As soon as we had risen, the old man came toward
me with a countenance beaming with joy. " This,"
said Mr. W., addressing me, " is *Uncle Harry*." He
reached out his hand and said: " Oh, why did my
God bring me here to-day, to hear what I have heard,
and see this salvation ? " I asked: " Are you as
ready to depart, Uncle Harry, as good old Simeon
was, of whom we read in this chapter ? " I shall
never forget his look of humble, joyful submission,
when he replied, " Just when it shall please my blessed Lord and Master." " You hope to go to heaven? "
" Through divine mercy, I do." " What is the foundation of that hope ? " " The righteousness of our
Lord and Saviour Jesus Christ."

On perceiving that I wished to converse with the
old man, Mr. W. said, with a kindness which showed
that he recognized Harry as a Christian brother, and

respected his age: "Come, take your seat again, Uncle Harry, and sit up near the fire." He accepted the invitation, and I entered into conversation, which afforded me higher pleasure than I ever enjoyed in the circles of fashion, beauty, wit and learning. I here send you some of the most interesting particulars.

"How old are you, Uncle Harry?" "Why, as nigh as I can tell, I am eighty-nine or thereabout." "Where were you born?" "At Port Tobacco, in Maryland." "And who had you to preach the gospel to you there?" "Ah, we had no preacher of the gospel there at that time." "Then it was after you left Port Tobacco that you embraced religion, was it?" "No, sir, it was while I lived there, and I will tell you how it was: A great many years ago there was one Dr. Whitefield, that travelled all through this country, preaching the gospel everywhere; I dare say you have heard of Dr. Whitefield, he was a most powerful preacher.

"Well, as I was saying, he went through Maryland, but his place of preaching was so far off that I did not hear of it until he was gone. But not long afterwards I met a man, an acquaintance of mine, who did hear him. He told me about the sermon; and what I heard opened my eyes to see that I was a poor lost sinner; and ever since that time I have been determined to seek Jesus as my Saviour, and to spend my life in His service."

Happy Whitefield! thought I, and greatly honored

of thy Master, who has used thee as His instrument in saving so many souls. " But," said I, " how old were you then ? " " Why, as nigh as I can guess, I was somewhere about sixteen or seventeen years old." " And have you never repented of this resolution? " " No, indeed, master; I have never repented of any thing, but that I have served my blessed Saviour so poorly."

" But have you not met many trials and difficulties by the way ? " " Yes, indeed, master; but out of them all the Lord has delivered me ; and having obtained help of God, I continue to this day : blessed be His name ; He never will leave me or forsake me; I have good hope of that."

" Well, how did you obtain religious instruction where you lived, as you say there was no preacher of the gospel in the neighborhood? " " Why, by the mercy of my God, I learned to read the Bible ; and that showed me the way to Jesus. But now I think of it, when the Roman Catholics heard that I was concerned about my soul, they sent for me, and tried hard to get me to join them.

" There was a priest at Port Tobacco, whose name was Mr. O'Neal; he talked to me a great deal. I remember he said to me one day, ' Harry, now you are concerned about your soul, you must come and join the Catholic church.' ' What for,' said I, ' Mr. O'Neal ? ' ' Because,' said he, ' it is the true church.' ' Then,' said I, ' if the Catholic church will lead me to Jesus, I will join it with all my heart, for that is all
10

I want;' and Mr. O'Neal said, 'If you will join the
church, I will warrant that you shall go to heaven.'
'How can you do that, Mr. O'Neal?' said I.

"Then he told me that a great many years ago our
Saviour came into the world, and He chose twelve
apostles, and made St. Peter their head; and the
Pope succeeded St. Peter; and so all that join the
Pope belong to the true church. 'Then,' said I,
'why, how do you know that, Mr. O'Neal?' 'Because,' said he, 'our Saviour told Peter, I give you the
keys of the kingdom of heaven; and whatsoever you
bind on earth shall be bound in heaven, and whatsoever you loose on earth shall be loosed in heaven.'

"And I said, 'The Lord knows how it is, Mr.
O'Neal; I am a poor ignorant creature, but it always
did seem to me that Peter was nothing but a man,
like the other apostles;' but Mr. O'Neal said, 'No,
he was the head and chief of the apostles; for our
Saviour said again, Thou art Peter, and on this rock
I will build My church; and the gates of hell shall
not prevail against it.' And I asked him, 'Now, do
you think Peter was that rock, Mr. O'Neal?' He
answered, 'To be sure he was;' and I said again,
'The Lord knows how it is; but it never did seem so
to me.

"'Now I think it was just so—when Peter said,
Thou art the Christ, the Son of the living God, our
Saviour told him, Thou *art Peter*,'" (while the old
man repeated the words, *Thou art Peter*, he pointed
his finger at me, and looked me directly in the face,

but as soon as he began the following part of the quotation he brought his hand briskly down to his knee, saying with emphasis, as he looked at himself), "'and upon this rock will I build My church; and that rock was Christ; for it is written in another place, Behold, I lay in Zion a chief corner-stone, elect, precious; and he that believeth on Him shall not be confounded; and that corner-stone is Christ.'

"Then Mr. O'Neal said to me, 'Why, Harry, where did you learn that?' I said, 'From my Bible.' 'Oh!' said he, 'you have no business with the Bible; it will confuse and frustrate you.' But I said, 'It tells me of my Saviour.' Then a gentleman, who was sitting by, said, 'Oh! you might as well let him alone, Mr. O'Neal; you cannot make anything of him;' and from that time I never had any desire to join the Roman Catholics."

The narrative, of the truth of which I could not entertain a moment's doubt, showed a promptness of reply and an acquaintance with the Scriptures which truly surprised me, and I remarked, "I suppose, Uncle Harry, you take great pleasure in reading the Bible?" "Ah, master! when I could read, it was the pleasure of my life. But I am old now; and my book is so rubbed that the print is dim, and I can scarcely make out to read a word."

On this, Mr. W. said, "Well, Uncle Harry, you shall have a new Bible. Do you call on Mr. ——, when you go down town, and he will give you a new one from the Bible Society." Harry bowed, and ex-

pressed gratitude for the kindness, but did not manifest as much pleasure as I expected, considering how
highly he professed to value the Bible.   While I was
wondering, and rather sorrowing on the account, I
observed the old man to be feeling, with an air of
embarrassment, in his pocket.

At length he pulled out an old tattered case, which
appeared to have been long in use, and observed,
" This new Bible will not be of much use to me,
because my spectacles are so bad that they help me
very little in reading."   With that he opened his
case, and showed a pair of spectacles of the cheapest
sort, of which one glass was broken, and the other so
scratched, that it was wonderful that he could see
through it at all.

Mr. · W. no sooner observed this than he said,
" Well, Uncle Harry, you must have a new pair ; do
call at Mr. ——'s store, and tell him to let you have
a pair suited to your age, and I will settle with him
about it."   On hearing this, Harry's eyes gleamed
with joy, and he exclaimed, " Thank God !   God
bless you, master !   Now I shall have comfort again
in reading the Bible."   And I never saw a happier,
or a more grateful countenance.

Presently, he said the wagon would soon call for
him to take him home, and he must go down town,
and be getting ready : on which he again thanked his
friend, and invoked a blessing on him and his family.
He then affectionately and respectfully took me by
the hand, and said, " I never saw you before, and I

never shall see you again in this world; but I love you as a minister of my blessed Lord and Master, and I hope that I shall meet you in the house above. Remember and pray for poor old Harry."

I squeezed his hand, and assured him of my affectionate remembrance, and requested that he would pray for me, and for the preachers of the Gospel generally. " Oh ! " said he, " may God Almighty bless all the dear ministers of Christ, and enable them to call many poor sinners to the dear Saviour ! Oh ! I do love to hear of souls coming to Christ; and it is my daily prayer—Thy kingdom come, and Thy will be done on earth, as it is done in heaven ! " With that the old man took leave.

I confess that I have often since wished to see him and hold communion with him. There was about him a spirit of piety and benevolence, of humble zeal and fervent hope, of meekness and submission, which I have rarely seen equalled. At the same time, there was a degree of intelligence, an extent of religious knowledge, which, in his condition, really surprised and delighted me.

I saw here one of the triumphs of divine grace. I was made to appreciate the value and the excellence of that religion which could take a poor slave, and so transform him, that he was well nigh fitted to be a companion of saints in light, and of just men made perfect. And since I saw him, I have often prayed that after the days of my wandering shall be over, and all the sufferings of my life shall be endured, I

may obtain a share in the rest, and a lot in the
inheritance, which I have no doubt are prepared for
Uncle Harry.

———

THE HOSPITABLE NEGRO WOMAN.

THE enterprising traveller, Mungo Park, was employed by the African Association to explore the
interior regions of Africa.   In this hazardous undertaking, he encountered many dangers and difficulties.
His wants were often supplied, and his distress allevi-
ated, by the kindness and compassion of negroes.   He
gives the following lively and interesting account of
the hospitable treatment he received from a poor
negro woman :

" Being arrived at Sego, the capital of the kingdom
of Bambarra, situated on the banks of the Niger, I
wished to pass over to that part of the town in which
the king resides ; but from the number of persons
eager to obtain a passage, I was under the necessity
of waiting two hours.   During this time the people
who had crossed the river carried information to
Mansong, the king, that a white man was waiting for
a passage, and was coming over to see him.

" He immediately sent over one of his chief men,
who informed me that the king could not possibly see
me until he knew what had brought me into this
country, and that I must not presume to cross the
river without the king's permission.   He therefore

advised me to lodge, for that night, in a distant village, to which he pointed, and said that in the morning he would give me further instruction how to conduct myself. This was very discouraging. However,
as there was no remedy, I set off for the village;
where I found, to my great mortification, that no
person would admit me into his house.

"From prejudices infused into their minds, I was
regarded with astonishment and fear; and I was
obliged to sit the whole day without victuals, in the
shade of a tree. The night threatened to be very
uncomfortable; the wind rose, and there was great
appearance of a heavy rain. The wild beasts too
were so numerous in the neighborhood, that I should
have been under the necessity of climbing up a tree,
and resting among the branches.

"About sunset, however, as I was preparing to
pass the night in this manner, and had turned my
horse loose, that he might graze at liberty, a negro
woman, returning from the labors of the field, stopped
to observe me; and perceiving that I was weary and
dejected, she inquired into my situation. I briefly
explained it to her; after which, with looks of great
compassion, she took up my saddle and bridle, and
told me to follow her. Having conducted me into
her hut, she lighted a lamp, spread a mat on the floor,
and told me I might remain there for the night.

"Finding I was very hungry, she went out to procure me something to eat; and returned in a short
time with a very fine fish, which, having caused it to

be half broiled upon some embers, she gave me for supper. The rites of hospitality being thus performed toward a stranger in distress, my worthy benefactress (pointing to the mat, and telling me I might sleep there without apprehension), called to the female part of her family, who had stood gazing on me all the while in fixed astonishment, to resume their task of spinning cotton ; in which they continued to employ themselves a great part of the night.

" They lightened their labor by songs, one of which was composed extempore ; for I was myself the subject of it. It was sung by one of the young women, the rest joining in a sort of .chorus. The air was sweet and plaintive, and the words, literally translated, were these : ' The winds roared, and the rain fell. The poor white man, faint and weary, came and sat under our tree. He has no mother to bring him milk, no wife to grind his corn.' *Chorus*: ' Let us pity the white man ; no mother has he to bring him milk, no wife to grind his corn.' *

" Trifling as these events may appear to the reader, they were to me affecting in the highest degree. I

---

* These simple and affecting sentiments have been very beautifully versified.

    1. The loud wind roar'd, the rain fell fast,
       The white man yielded to the blast.
       He sat him down beneath the tree,
       For weary, sad, and faint was he :
       And ah ! no wife's or mother's care,
       For him the milk or corn prepare.

was oppressed by such unexpected kindness, and sleep fled from my eyes. In the morning, I presented to my compassionate landlady two of the four brass buttons which remained on my waistcoat; the only recompense it was in my power to make her."

GRATITUDE IN A LIBERATED SLAVE.

SOME time in the year 1790 a member of the Manumission Society, residing on Golden Hill (now called John Street) in New York, observed, for a considerable time, his front porch to be scrubbed and sanded, every Seventh-day morning before the family were up.

CHORUS.

The white man shall our pity share—
Alas ! no wife's or mother's care
For him the milk or corn prepare.

2. The storm is o'er, the tempest past,
   And Mercy's voice has hush'd the blast;
   The wind is heard in whispers low,
   The white man far away must go ;
   But ever in his heart will bear
   Remembrance of the negro's care.

CHORUS.

Go, white man, go ; but with thee bear
The negro's wish, the negro's prayer,
Remembrance of the negro's care.

10*

He ordered a servant to watch, and ascertain to whom he was indebted for this singular mark of kindness.

At an early hour in the morning a colored woman was observed with her pail, brush, cloth, soap and sand, carefully performing her accustomed task. The domestic who had been on the watch followed her home, and requested to know her inducements for performing this service. Her reply was, "Massa got me free, and I can do no less than scrub off the stoop." A gratitude so genuine and untainted is rarely found among the most polished and refined minds.

AGNES MORRIS.

ANOTHER narrative, respecting a dying woman, displays a faith so strong, a hope so full of immortality, as may lead the Christian reader to exclaim, " Let my last hours be like those of this poor slave." Agnes Morris, a poor negro woman, sent a pressing request to Mrs. Thwaites, a lady residing in Antigua, to visit her: she was in the last stage of dropsy.

This poor creature ranked among the lowest class of slaves. Her all consisted of a little wattled* hut and a few clothes. Mrs. Thwaites, finding her at the commencement of her illness in a very destitute condition, mentioned her case to a friend, who gave her a coat. When she paid her last visit, on her entering the door, Agnes exclaimed, " Missis ! you come !

---

* Plaited twigs.

This tongue can't tell what Jesus do for me! Me call my Saviour day and night; and He come "—laying her hand on her breast—"He comfort me here."

On being asked if she was sure of going to heaven when she died, she answered, "Yes, me sure. Me see de way clear, and shine before me "—looking and pointing upward with a smiling face. "If di dis minute, Jesus will take me home, me ready." Some hymns being sung, she was in a rapture of joy; and in reference to the words of one of them, exclaimed, "For me—for me—poor sinner!"—lifting up her swelled hands—"what a glory! what a glory!"

Seeing her only daughter weeping, she said, "What you cry for? No cry—follow Jesus—He will take care of you." And turning to Mrs. Thwaites, she said, "Missis, show um de path:" meaning the path to heaven. Many other expressions fell from her of a similar nature, to the astonishment of those who heard her. It was understood she continued praying and praising God to her latest breath.

This poor creature was destitute of all earthly comforts. Her bed was a board, with a few plantain leaves over it. How many of these outcasts will be translated from outward wretchedness to realms of glory, there to mingle with the blessed, and sing praises to Him who lives for ever!

EXTRAORDINARY EXERTIONS TO OBTAIN LIBERTY.

THAT human being who would run the gauntlet for freedom so desperately as the poor African appears to have done, whose story is given below, surely should never again be brought under the lash of a taskmaster. The captain of a vessel from North Carolina called upon the police for advisement respecting a slave he had unconsciously brought away in his vessel, under the following curious circumstances:

Three or four days after he had got to sea he began to be haunted every hour with tones of distress seemingly proceeding from a human voice in the very lowest part of the vessel. A particular scrutiny was finally instituted, and it was concluded that the creature, whatever or whoever it might be, must be confined down in the run under the cabin floor; and on boring a hole with an auger, and demanding, '*Who's there?*' a feeble voice responded, '*Poor negro, massa!*' It was clear enough then that some runaway negro had hid himself there before they sailed, trusting to Providence for his ultimate escape.

Having discovered him, however, it was impossible to give him relief, for the captain had stowed even the cabin so completely full of cotton as but just to leave room for a small table for himself and the mate to eat on; and as for unloading at sea, that was pretty much out of the question. Accordingly, there he had to lie, stretched at full length, for the tedious interval of *thirteen days*, till the vessel arrived in port and unloaded, receiving his food and drink through the auger hole.

The fellow's story is, now he is released, that, being determined to get away from slavery, he supplied himself with eggs, and biscuit, and some jugs of water, which latter he was just on the point of depositing in his lurking-place, when he discovered the captain at a distance coming on board, and had to hurry down as fast as possible and leave them; that he lived on nothing but his eggs and biscuit till discovered by the captain, not even getting a drop of water, except what he had the good fortune to catch in his hand one day, when a vessel of water in the cabin was overset, during a squall, and some of it ran down through the cracks of the floor over him.

WILLIAM BOWEN.

DIED, near Mount Holly, New Jersey, 12th of sixth month, 1824, in the 90th year of his age, William Bowen, a man of color. The deceased was one of those who have demonstrated the truth of that portion of Scripture that, "in every nation, he that feareth God and worketh righteousness is accepted with Him."

He was concerned in early life to do justly, love

mercy, and walk humbly with his God; and by closely attending to the light of Christ, and faithfully abiding under the operation of that blessed spirit of Divine Grace in his soul, he was enabled not only to bear many precious testimonies, through his life, but to bring forth those fruits of the Spirit which redound to the glory of God and to the salvation of the soul.

He was an exemplary member of the religious Society of Friends. As he lived so he died, a rare pattern of a self-denying follower of Jesus Christ. He had no apparent disease either of body or mind; and as he expressed himself, but a short time before his death, "he felt nothing but weakness," which continued to increase until he gently breathed his last, and no doubt entered into his Heavenly Father's rest. "Mark the perfect man, and behold the upright, for the end of that man is peace."

ANTHONY BENEZET.

DIED, on the 3d of fifth month, 1784, Anthony Benezet, aged 71 years, a member of the Society of Friends. It was a day of sorrow. The afflicted widow, the unprotected orphan, and the poor of all descriptions, had lost the sympathetic mind of Benezet. Society lamented the extinguishment of the brilliant light of his philanthropy.

The wandering tribes in the American wilderness,

and the oppressed Africans, were indeed bereft; for his willing pen and tongue had ceased forever to portray the history of their injuries, or plead for the establishment of their rights, before the sons of men.

At the interment of his remains, in Friends' burial ground in Philadelphia, was the greatest concourse of people that had ever been witnessed on such an occasion; being a collection of all ranks and professions among the inhabitants; thus manifesting the universal esteem in which he was held.

Among others who paid that last tribute of respect were many hundred colored people, testifying, by their attendance and by their tears, the grateful sense they entertained of his pious efforts in their behalf. Having no children, by his will he bequeathed his estate to his wife during her natural life. At her decease, he directed several small sums to be paid to poor and obscure persons.

The residue he devised in trust to the overseers of the public school, " to hire and employ a religious-minded person or persons to teach a number of negro, mulatto or Indian children to read, write, arithmetic, plain accounts, needle-work, etc. And it is my particular desire, founded on the experience I have had in that service, that, in the choice of such tutor, special care may be taken to prefer an industrious, careful person, of true piety, who may be or become suitably qualified, who would undertake the service from a principle of charity, to one more highly learned not equally disposed."

He also bequeathed, as a special legacy, the sum of fifty pounds to the Society in Pennsylvania for the promotion of the abolition of slavery. Thus closed the life of this great and good man. Dispensing his blessings with his own hand, he was too liberal to be a man of wealth. He was a native of France; and in the ancient records of his family are exhibited evidences of religious character in his predecessors.

Connected with the demise of his grandfather, the event is said to be, "to the great affliction of his children, and the universal regret of his relatives and friends, for he was a model of virtue and purity, and lived in the constant fear of God." Attached to the birth-note of his grandson Anthony, are these expressions: "May God bless him, in making him a partaker of his mercies." Though virtue is not hereditary, it must be admitted that example is powerful.

Among the productions of Anthony Benezet's pen, was, "An historical account of Guinea, its situation, produce, and the general disposition of its inhabitants; with an inquiry into the rise and progress of the slave trade, its nature, and calamitous effects."

Note from the Memoirs of A. Benezet.

The influence of this work, in giving an impulse to the mind of the indefatigable and benevolent Thomas Clarkson, whose exertions contributed so much toward bringing about the abolition of the slave trade by the British Parliament, is certainly remarkable. In the year 1785, Dr. Peckard, vice-chancellor of the University of Cambridge, proposed to the senior Bachelors of Arts, of whom Clarkson was one, the following question for a Latin dissertation : viz. (in English), " Is it right to make slaves of others against their will ? "

Having in the former year gained a prize for the best Latin dissertation, he resolved to maintain the classical reputation he had acquired by applying himself to the subject; but it was one with which he was by no means familiar, and he was at a loss what authors to consult respecting it; " when going by accident," he says, " into a friend's house, I took up a newspaper then lying on the table.

" One of the articles which attracted my notice, was an advertisement of Anthony Benezet's historical account of Guinea. I soon left my friend and his paper, and, to lose no time, hastened to London to buy it. In this precious book I found almost all I wanted." The information furnished by Benezet's book encouraged him to complete his essay, which was rewarded with the first prize; and from that moment, Clarkson's mind became interested with the great subject of the abolition.

EXTRAORDINARY MUNIFICENCE.

FROM THE GENIUS OF UNIVERSAL EMANCIPATION—
1825.

A PARAGRAPH has lately gone the round of the papers announcing that a gentleman of Virginia had emancipated *upwards of eighty slaves*, and chartered a vessel to send them at his own expense to Hayti, but without giving the name of the author of so distinguished an act of munificence.

" We think it due to justice," says the Norfolk Herald, " to supply this deficiency, and to add the following facts, which have been communicated to us by gentlemen familiar with them, as well as by Captain Russell, one of the owners of the brig Hannah and Elizabeth, of Baltimore, the vessel chartered.

" The gentleman who has thus distinguished himself, is David Minge, of Charles City county, living near Sandy Point, on James River. Captain Russell informs us that there were put on board the Hannah and Elizabeth eighty-seven colored people of different ages, from three months to forty years, being all the slaves Mr. Minge owned, except two old men, whom he had likewise manumitted, but who, being past service, he retains and supports them.

" The value of these negroes, at the prices now going, might be estimated at about twenty-six thousand dollars ! and Mr. Minge expended, previous to their embarkation, about twelve hundred dollars in purchasing ploughs, hoes, iron, and other articles of husbandry for them; besides providing them with several suits of clothes to each, provisions, groceries, cooking utensils, and everything which he supposed they might require for their comfort during the passage, and for their use after their arrival out. He also paid sixteen hundred dollars for the charter of the vessel.

"But Mr. Minge's munificence does not end here. On the bank of the river, as they were about to go on board, he had a peck of dollars brought down, and calling them around him, under a tree, he distributed the hoard among them, in such sums, and under such regulations, that each individual did, or would, receive seven dollars.

"By this provision, Mr. Minge thought his emigrants would be enabled to commence the cultivation of the soil immediately after their arrival, without being dependent on President Boyer for any favor whatever, unless the permission to improve the government lands be so considered.

"Mr. Minge is about twenty-four or twenty-five years of age, unmarried, and unencumbered in every respect; possesses an ample fortune, and received the benefits of a collegiate education at Harvard University.

"We have heard of splendid sacrifices at the shrine of philanthropy; aged men, on quitting the stage of mortal existence, have bequeathed large endowments to public charities, and princely legacies to religious and moral institutions. But where shall we find an instance of the kind attributable to a man of Mr. Minge's age? The case, we believe, is without a parallel."

———

TEMPTATION RESISTED AND HONESTY REWARDED.

FROM DILLWYN'S ANECDOTES.

A POOR chimney sweeper's boy was employed at the house of a lady of rank to sweep the chimney of the room in which she usually dressed. When finding himself on the hearth of a richly-furnished dressing-room, and perceiving no one there, he waited a few moments to take a view of the beautiful things in the apartment.

A gold watch, richly set with diamonds, particularly caught his attention, and he could not forbear taking it in his hand. Immediately the wish rose in his mind, "Ah! if you had such a one!" After a pause, he said to himself, "But if I take it I shall be a thief; and yet," continued he, "nobody would know it; nobody sees me—nobody! Does not God see me, who is present everywhere?" Overcome by these thoughts, a cold shivering seized him. "No," said he, putting down the watch, "I would much rather be poor, and keep my good conscience, than rich and become a rascal." At these words he hastened back into the chimney.

The lady, who was in the room adjoining, having overheard the conversation with himself, sent for him the next morning, and thus accosted him : "My little friend, why did you not take the watch yesterday ? " The boy fell on his knees, speechless and astonished. "I heard every thing you said," continued her lady-ship; "thank God for enabling you to resist this temptation, and be watchful over yourself for the future : from this moment you shall be in my service : I will both maintain and clothe you: nay, more, pro-cure you good instruction, which will assist to guard you from the danger of similar temptations."

The boy burst into tears ; he was anxious to express his gratitude, but could not. The lady strictly kept her promise, and had the pleasure of seeing this poor *chimney-sweeper* grow up a good, pious and intelligent man.

An Indian, being among his white neighbors, asked for a little tobacco to smoke, and one of them, having some loose in his pocket, gave him a handful. The day following the Indian came back, inquiring for the donor, saying he had found a quarter of a dollar among the tobacco. Being told that as it was given him he might as well keep it, he answered, pointing to his breast, "I got a good man, and a bad man here, and the good man say, 'It ain't yours ; you must return it to its owner : ' the bad man say, 'Why, he gave it to you, and it is your own now : ' the good man say, 'That's not right; the tobacco is yours, not the money :' the bad man say, 'Never mind, you got it, go buy some dram:' the good man say, 'No, you must not do so :' so I don't know what to do, and I think I go to sleep ; but the good man and the bad keep talking all night, and trouble me; and now I bring the money back I feel good."

Another Indian related, that, having got some money, he was, on his way home, tempted to stop at a tavern and buy some rum; " But, " said he, pointing to his breast, " I have a good boy and a bad boy here; and the good boy say, ' John, don't you stop there : the bad one say, ' Poh, John, never mind, you love a good dram:' the good boy say, 'No, John, you know what a fool you made yourself when you got drunk there before, don't do so again.' When I come to the tavern, the bad boy say, ' Come, John, take one dram; it won't hurt you :' the good one say, ' No, John, if you take one dram, then you take another:' then I don't know what to do, and the good boy say, ' Run, John, hard as you can '—so I run away, and then, be sure, I feel very glad."

THE GOOD OLD INDIAN.

CAPTAIN JAMES SMITH relates, that he was taken prisoner by the Indians in the year 1755, and lived several years among them. At one time, he lived with

an old man named Tecaughretanego, and his little son,
Nunganny; they were quite alone, and there were not
any inhabitants for many miles around. The old man
was too lame to go out hunting; it was winter; they
had no victuals; the snow was on the ground, and so
frozen as to make a great noise when walked on,
which frightened away the deer, and the captain
could not shoot anything for some time.

He says: "After I had hunted two days without
eating anything, and had very short allowance for
some days before, I returned late in the evening,
faint and weary. When I came into our hut, the old
man asked what success. I told him not any. He
asked me if I was not very hungry. I replied that
the keen appetite seemed in some measure abated, but
I was both faint and weary.

"He commanded his little son to bring me something to eat; and he brought me a kettle with some
bones and broth. After eating a few mouthfuls my
appetite violently returned, and I thought the victuals had a most agreeable relish, though it was only
fox and wildcat bones, which lay about the ground,
which the ravens and turkey-buzzards had picked;
these Nunganny had collected, and boiled until the
sinews that remained on them would strip off. I
speedily finished my allowance, and when I had ended
my *sweet* repast the old man asked me how I felt. I
told him I was much refreshed.

"He then handed me his pipe and pouch, and told
me to take a good smoke. I did so. He then said

he had something of importance to tell me, if I was now composed and ready to hear it. I told him I was ready to hear him. He said, 'The reason why I deferred my speech till now is because few men are in a right humor to hear good talk when they are very hungry, as they are then generally fretful and discomposed; but as you now appear to enjoy calmness and serenity of mind, I will communicate to you the thoughts of my heart, and those things I know to be true.

"'Brother, as you have lived with the white people, you have not had the same advantage of knowing that the great Being above feeds His people, and gives them their meat in due season, as we Indians have, who are frequently out of provisions, and yet are wonderfully supplied, and that so frequently that it is evidently the hand of the Great Spirit that does this; whereas, the white people have commonly large stocks of tame cattle, that they can kill when they please; and they also have barns and cribs, filled with grain, and therefore have not the same opportunity of seeing that they are supported by the Ruler of heaven and earth.

"'Brother, I know you are now afraid that we will all perish with hunger, but you have no just reason to fear this. I have been young, but I am now old. I have been frequently under the like circumstances that we now are, and some time or another in almost every year of my life; yet I have hitherto been supported, and my wants supplied in time of need.

"' Brother, the Good Spirit sometimes suffers us to be in want, in order to teach us our dependence on Him, and to let us know that we are to love and serve Him; likewise to know the worth of the favors that we receive, and also to make us thankful.

"' Brother, be assured that you will be supplied with food, and that just in the right time: but you must continue diligent in the use of means: go to sleep, and rise early in the morning, and go a hunting—be strong, and exert yourself, like a man, and the Great Spirit will direct your way.' "

The captain was thus encouraged to try again the next morning, though much disheartened and extremely hungry. He went a great distance before he could shoot anything; but at length he shot a buffalo cow; thus finding, as the good old Indian had said, that the Great Spirit had enabled him to provide for them just at the time of their distress.

FAITH OF A POOR BLIND WOMAN.

A PERSON going to see a very aged woman of color, found a respectable-looking white girl sitting by her, reading the Bible for her. On inquiring of the old woman whether she could ever read, the visitor was answered, "Oh, yes, mistress, and I used to read a great deal in that book (pointing to a Bible very much worn that lay on the table), but now I am most

11

blind, and the good girls read for me ; but by and by,
when I get on Zion's hill, I shall then see as well as
anybody."

The poor of this world are often found rich in faith,
and their confidence in the wisdom and goodness of a
bountiful Creator, strong.   How frequently, on visit·
ing the abodes of the aged and the infirm, do we find
this verified : one saying, when something is handed
her, " The Lord has sent me this ; "—another, " The
Lord put it into my heart to be industrious, and lay
up something for old age," etc.

AFRICAN SCHOOLS IN NEW YORK.

THE Clarkson Association, for instructing adult
females of color, commenced in the spring of 1811,
and was conducted ten or twelve years by a number
of young ladies of the Society of Friends.   This was
the first institution that came under the appellation
of Sabbath-school in this city, where there are now so
many.

It was taught on that day, because those people
had generally more leisure to attend than on other
days of the week ; but these benevolent ladies soon
appropriated also one afternoon in the middle of the
week, for such as were at liberty to attend.   There
were a considerable number of aged women, as well as
those in the prime of life, who learned to read, and

rejoiced greatly in the acquisition. There were also schools kept by young men, for adults of color of the other sex.

"There is one remarkable fact connected with the effects of this excellent school upon the moral condition of the colored people. At every term of the Court of Sessions in this city, there are many colored persons convicted of crimes, and sent to the State prison or penitentiary. This school has now been in operation a number of years, and several thousands of scholars have received the benefits of a good thorough English education, *and but three persons who have been educated here have been convicted in our criminal courts.*"

Several girls, who have received their education at this school, have gone with their parents to Hayti, where they will be capable of teaching schools, and may be of singular benefit. Two interesting letters, written in a very fair intelligible hand, by one of these girls about fourteen years old, have been received by E. J. Cox; extracts from which are here subjoined.

"REPUBLIC OF HAYTI,
"CITY OF ST. DOMINGO, Sept. 29, 1824.

"DEAR TEACHER :—With pleasure I hasten to inform you of our safe arrival in St. Domingo, after a passage of twenty-one days. Mother and myself were very much afflicted with sea-sickness for about nine or ten days, but after that we enjoyed a little of the pleasures of our voyage.

" On our arrival, we were conducted by the captain of the port to the governor's house, where we were received by him with all the friendship that he could have received us with had we been intimately acquainted for years. After informing him of our intention of residing on the island, we were conducted to the residence of the second general in command, where we had our names registered.

" From thence we went to see the principal chapel in the city; to give a description of which, it requires a far abler pen than mine; " (she, however, mentions many particulars;) " but you cannot form an idea of it, unless you could see for yourself. After we had viewed the church throughout, we were conducted to our lodging, at which place we are at present. Since we have been here, my sampler and bench-cover have been seen by a number of ladies and gentlemen, and have been very much admired by all who have seen them.

" Dear teacher, notwithstanding we are hundreds of miles from each other, I hope you will not think that I shall forget you, or those kind friends (I mean the trustees), who have been so kind to me : for had it not been for them and yourself, perhaps I never should have known one half what I do, as respects my education; for which, for them and you, to God I shall offer up my humble prayers for your welfare, both in this life and that which is to come.

" I am, with respect, yours,

" SERENA M. BALDWIN."

THE INJURED AFRICANS.

FROM THE NEW YORK OBSERVER—1826.

IN our paper of the 21st of January we inserted a communication from a correspondent giving an account of an aged colored woman who emigrated with her husband from New Orleans to this city last summer, bringing with her another colored woman whom she had rescued from slavery at the expense of *her little all*. The object of these poor people in coming to New York was simply to enjoy the privileges of the gospel without interruption.

A benevolent gentleman of our acquaintance whose feelings were much interested in the account which we published, and who has since repeatedly visited this interesting family, has put into our hands the following particulars of their history for publication. The name of the husband is *Reuben*, that of his wife, *Betsey*, and that of their companion, *Fanny*.

Reuben Madison, the husband, was born in Virginia, near Port Royal, about the year 1781. His parents, and all his connections in this country, were slaves. His father died when he was about seven years old. His mother is now living in Kentucky, enjoying freedom in her old age, through the filial regard of Reuben, who purchased her liberty for seventy dollars. She is seriously disposed, but not a professor of religion.

He has now eight brothers and sisters living in
Frankfort, Franklin county, Kentucky, all slaves, and
all, excepting one, members of a Baptist church in
that place.   About a year after his conversion Reuben was married to a slave, who had been kidnapped
in Maryland and sold to a planter in his neighborhood.   She was also hopefully pious.

While they lived together she became the mother of
two children ; but about four years after their marriage she and one of the children, aged eight months,
were sold without his knowledge, and transported to a
distant Spanish territory, and with so much secrecy
that he had no opportunity even to bid her a last farewell.   " This," said he, " was the severest trial of my
life, a sense of sin only excepted.   I mourned and
cried, and would not be comforted.

" After several months, however, the hope of meeting her and my children again in the kingdom of God,
when we should never be separated, together with a
promise from my master that I should at some future
time go to see her, in some measure allayed my grief,
and permitted me to enjoy the consolations of religion."
The other child is now a slave in Kentucky, though the
father has often endeavored in vain to purchase his
freedom.

About six years since, having hired his time of his
master for five years previous, at 120 dollars a year,
Reuben succeeded, by trafficking in rags, and in other
ways, in collecting a sum sufficient for the purchase of
his own freedom, for which he paid 700 dollars, and

not only so, but he was enabled, with his surplus earnings, to build a brick house, and to provide it with
convenient accommodations. By the dishonesty of
his former master, however, all was taken from
him.

Thus stripped of his property, he left Kentucky and
went to New Orleans, that he might learn something
from his wife, and, if possible, find and redeem her;
but he only succeeded in gaining the painful intelligence that she was dead. He there formed an acquaintance with his present wife, whose former name
was Betsey Bond, and they were soon married. The
circumstances of her life were briefly these :

Betsey was born a slave, near Hobb's Hole, Essex
county, Virginia, about 1763, and was married to a
slave at about the age of twenty years. By him she
had three children, one of which, together with
her husband, died a few years after their marriage.
Soon after their death, she was led to reflect on her
lost state as a sinner, and after about seven months of
deep anxiety was enabled, as she trusts, to resign herself into the hands of her Saviour, and experience
those consolations which He deigns to grant to the
broken-hearted penitent.

She gained the confidence and attachment of her
mistress, who treated her with much kindness, and she
was married to a pious servant of the family, where
she remained about nine years. At the close of this
period a planter from the vicinity of Natchez, coming
to Alexandria in Virginia, where she then lived, for

slaves, she was sold, and carried, with eight others, to his plantation, leaving her husband behind.

Her new master treated her with great severity, and she was compelled to labor almost incessantly every day of the week, Sabbath not excepted. With this man she lived nineteen years. He then died, and left his slaves, by will, to another planter, who also dying soon after, she was again sold and transported to New Orleans, where she arrived about the year 1812.

At the end of two years this master also died; and when his slaves were about to be sold, Betsey succeeded with some difficulty in hiring her time, and in a little more than a year, by washing and other labor, she acquired sufficient property to purchase her freedom, for which she paid 250 dollars. Her youngest son and his wife being also slaves in New Orleans, she hoped to obtain, by her industry and economy, money sufficient to purchase them also; but their master refused to part with them.

Several years after a large number of slaves were brought to New Orleans from Virginia, and were about to be offered for sale, and Fanny was among the number. Having accidentally become acquainted with her, previous to the sale, and finding her a sister in Christ, Betsey's feelings were deeply interested, and she resolved to purchase her, and to treat her not as a slave, but as a child and companion.

This determination she communicated to Fanny, and with the aid of a gentleman she succeeded in accomplishing her object. The price was 250 dollars. She paid 200, *her all*, and obtained a short credit for the remainder. Soon after this her present husband, coming to New Orleans, as before stated, they were married, and the payment for Fanny was then completed.

By their united industry they were soon able to build a comfortable house, in which they set apart a room for religious purposes. Here they assembled with others every Sabbath, for the worship of God. But being constantly exposed to disturbance in their worship, they felt a great desire to go to a free State, where they might enjoy religious privileges unmolested; where they could unite with Christian friends in social prayer and conversation, without a soldier, with a drawn sword stationed at their door.

They fixed upon New York as the desired asylum; and having arranged their concerns, rented their house, and collected their effects, they engaged and paid their passage, which was seventy dollars, and sailed from New Orleans about the 12th of July, 1825, with pleasing anticipations, for a land of freedom and religious privileges.

They suffered much on the voyage, through the cruelty of the captain; being exposed without shelter, during the whole of the passage, either on deck or in the longboat. In consequence of this exposure, both of the women were taken sick; and in this condition they arrived at New York, and were landed on the

11*

wharf in a land of strangers, their money almost expended, and none to commiserate their sufferings.

After a few days, however, Reuben succeeded in obtaining a miserable cellar in Chapel Street, at sixty dollars annual rent, where he remained for some time, supporting the family in their sickness, by his labor as a shoemaker, and by the sale of some of his effects.

On his arrival at this port his first act was to grant entire freedom to Fanny, giving her liberty to live with him, or to go where she pleased. She chose to remain with him ; and she assisted in the support of the family by washing and other labor, and nursed her mistress, who was evidently declining with the consumption, occasioned doubtless by the severity of her treatment on the passage from New Orleans.

Not being able to pay their rent in advance, owing to their sickness and other expenses, their landlord compelled them to quit their residence ; and they have since been obliged to put up with still more miserable accommodations in a cellar in Elm Street.

They appeared to put their trust and confidence in God, and expressed their entire belief that all their trials were designed for their good. They seemed to be one in sentiment and feeling, and to manifest a spirituality of mind rarely to be found. Every little attention was most gratefully received, and the best of blessings were implored on him who bestowed it.

With some assistance from the benevolent, and with what they may receive from New Orleans for rent, it is believed they may be provided with a comfortable

house, and be introduced to those privileges which they
so ardently desire. No one of the family can read,
though they are all desirous to learn, and from a little
attention which their friends have given them it appears that they may be taught without difficulty.

It is an affecting thought, that the wrongs of this
poor woman, which commenced at her birth, and were
inflicted without interruption during the long years of
slavery, still followed her on her passage to the land
of freedom, and have been finally consummated in this
city, the city of her hopes, her fancied asylum from
the oppressor.

HENRY BOYD.

FROM THE ANTI-SLAVERY RECORD.

HENRY BOYD was born a slave in Kentucky. Of
imposing stature, well-knit muscles, and the countenance of one of nature's noblemen. At the age of
eighteen he had so far won the confidence of his
master, that he not only consented to sell him the
right and title to his freedom, but gave him his own
time to earn the money.

With a general pass from his master, Henry made
his way to the Kenhawa salt works, celebrated as the
place where Senator Ewing, of Ohio, chopped out his
education with his axe! And there, too, with his axe,
did Henry Boyd chop out his *liberty*. By performing

double labor, he got double wages. In the daytime he swung his axe upon the wood, and for half the night he tended the boiling salt-kettles, sleeping the other half by their side.

After having accumulated a sufficient sum, he returned to his master and paid it over for his freedom. He next applied himself to learn the trade of a carpenter and joiner. Such was his readiness to acquire the use of tools, that he soon qualified himself to receive the wages of a journeyman. In Kentucky prejudice does not forbid master mechanics to teach colored men their trades.

He now resolved to quit the dominions of slavery and try his fortunes in a free State, and accordingly directed his steps to the city of Cincinnati. The journey reduced his purse to the last *quarter of a dollar;* but, with his tools on his back and the consciousness of his ability to use them, he entered the city with a light heart. Little did he dream of the reception he was to meet. There was work enough to be done in his line, but no master workman would employ a colored man.

Day after day did Henry Boyd offer his services from shop to shop, but as often was he repelled, generally with insult, and once with a kick. At last, he found the shop of an Englishman, too recently arrived to understand the grand peculiarity of American feeling. This man put a plane into his hand, and asked him to make proof of his skill. "This is in bad order," said Boyd, and with that he gave the instrument certain nice professional knocks with the hammer, till he brought it to suit his practised eye.

"Enough," said the Englishman; "I see you can use tools." Boyd, however, proceeded to dress a board in a very able and workmanlike manner, while the journeymen from a long line of benches gathered around with looks that bespoke a deep personal interest in the matter. "You may go to work," said the master of the shop, right glad to employ so good a workman. The words had no sooner left his mouth than his American journeymen, unbuttoning their aprons, called, as one man, for the settlement of their wages.

"What! what!" said the amazed Englishman, "what does this mean?" "It means that we will not work with a *nigger*," replied the journeymen. "But he is a first-rate workman." "But we won't stay in the same shop with a *nigger*; we are not in the habit of working with *niggers*." "Then I will build a shanty outside, and he shall work in that." "No, no; we won't work for a *boss* who employs *niggers*. Pay us up, and we'll be off." The poor master of the shop turned with a despairing look to Boyd— "You see how it is, my friend; my workmen will all leave me. I am sorry for it, but I can't hire you."

Even at this repulse our adventurer did not despair. There might still be mechanics in the outskirts of the city who had too few journeymen to be bound by their prejudices. His quarter of a dollar had long since disappeared, but, by carrying a traveller's trunk

or turning his hand to any chance job, he contrived
to exist till he had made application to every carpenter and joiner in the city and its suburbs. *Not one
would employ him.* By this time, the iron of prejudice, more galling than anything he had ever known
of slavery, had entered his soul.

He walked down to the river's bank below the city,
and throwing himself upon the ground, gave way to
an agony of despair. He had found himself the object
of universal contempt; his plans were all frustrated,
his hopes dashed, and his dear-bought freedom made
of no effect! By such trials, weak minds are pros-
trated in abject and slavish servility, and stronger
ones are made the enemies and depredators of society ;
it is only the highest class of moral heroes that come
off like gold from the furnace.

Of this class, however, was Henry Boyd. Recover-
ing from his dejection, he surveyed the brawny muscles that strung his Herculean frame. A new design
rushed into his mind, and new resolution filled his
heart. He sprang upon his feet and walked firmly
and rapidly towards the city, doubtless with aspira-
tions that might have suited the words of the poet:

> " Thy spirit, *Independence*, let me share,
>   Lord of the lion heart and eagle eye."

The first object which attracted his "eagle eye," on
reaching the city, was one of the huge river boats
laden with pig iron, drawn up to the landing. The
captain of this craft was just inquiring of the merchant

who owned its contents for a hand to assist in unloading it. "I am the very fellow for you," said Boyd, stripping off his coat, rolling up his sleeves, and laying hold of the work. "Yes, sure enough, that *is* the very fellow for you," said the merchant.

The resolution and alacrity of Boyd interested him exceedingly, and during the four or five days in which a flotilla of boats were discharging their cargoes of pig iron with unaccustomed despatch, he became familiar with his history, with the exception of all that pertained to his trade, which Boyd thought proper to keep to himself. In consequence, our adventurer next found himself promoted to the portership of the merchant's store, a post which he filled to great satisfaction.

He had a hand and a head for everything, and an occasion was not long wanting to prove it. A joiner was engaged to erect a counter, but failing, by a drunken frolic, the merchant was disappointed and vexed. Rather in passion than in earnest, he turned to his faithful porter: "Here, Henry, you can do almost anything, why can't *you* do this job?" "Perhaps I could, sir, if I had my tools and the stuff," was the reply. "Your tools!" exclaimed the merchant in surprise, for till now he knew nothing of his trade.

Boyd explained that he had learned the trade of a carpenter and joiner, and had no objection to try the job. The merchant handed him the money, and told him to make as good a counter as he could. The work was done with such promptitude, judgment and finish

that his employer broke off a contract for the erection
of a large frame warehouse, which he was about clos-
ing with the same mechanic who had disappointed him
in the matter of the counter, and gave the job to
Henry.

The money was furnished, and Boyd was left to
procure the materials and *boss* the job at his own discretion. This he found no difficulty in doing, and
what is remarkable, among the numerous journeymen
whom he employed, were some of the very men who
took off their aprons at his appearance in the Englishman's shop ! The merchant was so much pleased with
his new warehouse, that he proceeded to set up the intelligent builder in the exercise of his trade in the city.

Thus Henry Boyd found himself raised at once almost beyond the reach of the prejudice which had
well-nigh crushed him.   He built houses and accumulated property.   White journeymen and appren-
tices were glad to be in his employment, and to *sit at
his table.*   He is now a wealthy mechanic, living in
his own house in Cincinnati ; and his enemies who
have tried to supplant him have as good reason as his
friends to know that he is a man of sound judgment
and a most vigorous intellect.

Without having received a day's schooling in his
life, Henry Boyd is well read in history, has an extensive and accurate knowledge of geography, is an excellent arithmetician, and is remarkable for his morality, generosity, and all those traits which mark a noble character.

QUAMINO BUCCAN,

A PIOUS METHODIST.

QUAMINO was born in the vicinity of New Brunswick, New Jersey, in 1762, and was a slave. In his ninth year he was hired for a term of years to a person named Schenk, who employed him as a house-servant, and who soon after removing to Poughkeepsie, New York, took the lad with him. The unsettled state of the country during the Revolutionary War, prevented communication with his old master, and Quamino had no hope of seeing his former friends; but in his eightieth year he was informed that his master had sent for him. On his return to New Jersey his old associates had so grown that he felt like a stranger in his old home.

When nearing the age of manhood he was steady in attending religious meetings, walking several miles through all kinds of weather. His own account of his motive in going was that he "liked to have the name of being a good boy." But whatever his motive in going, the meetings were a blessing to him. One Sabbath evening on reaching home he went to the barn, where, after earnest exercise in prayer, he slept upon the straw. Very early in the morning he went into the field to work, first kneeling by the fence. Being in great distress, the gracious words of the Saviour deeply impressed him: "*Let not your heart be troubled. Ye believe in God, believe also in Me.*"

Yielding his whole heart and all his powers to Him
who was calling for the sacrifice, he felt that he received the unspeakable gift.

He went to his work; "and oh," said he, "everything was glorious around me—everything seemed to
be praising God."

The change which had come over the boy was conspicuous to all around him; he was quiet and
diligent in attention to all his duties. From this
time Quamino understood the nature of that peace
"which passeth all understanding." On the Sabbath
he would get the carriage ready, and when his master
had started he would walk several miles across the
fields to the Methodist meeting, but always left before
the conclusion of the services, as, if not at home in
time to take the horses when the family arrived, he
was sure to be found fault with, if not punished.

At the age of twenty-six he married Sarah, a slave
on a neighboring place. She was soon sold to a distance of five miles, and for some years they only met
once a week. One Sabbath morning he went to see
her, and found that she and her infant had been sold,
leaving her little son, a boy nearly four years old.
She now had a hard master; but, through the efforts
of her husband, she was purchased by a neighbor,
and, at length, by the removal of this purchaser,
Quamino induced his second master (to whom he had
been sold when about thirty years old) to buy her.
Afterwards Dr. Griffith bought Quamino for $250, and
Sarah for $150.

At the death of Dr. Griffith his goods and chattels (including his slaves) were advertised to be sold at public auction. The sale commenced, and Quamino and Sarah became objects of much attention; but a letter was received from Wm. Griffith, the son and executor of the late master, directing that everything should be sold to the highest bidder except the carriage and horse, and that with these Quamino should bring Sarah to Burlington. "Oh, my dear friend," said he in narrating it, "you do not know how I felt."

Wm. Griffith was not only an eminent lawyer but bore a part in originating the New Jersey Abolition Society. For this excellent man, whose "record is on high," Quamino worked to the best of his ability. One day, as he was at work in the garden, he heard his name called, and seeing his master beside him, he modestly said, "Sir!" We will describe what took place in the good old man's words. Says he:

"Would you like to be free?" and I said, "I don't know, sir." He stood in silence a little while, and I went on working the same as before. At last he said, 'I've made up my mind to give you free;' and says I, 'you give me free, master?' Oh, it all came on me so unexpected! And then he up and told me all how he would do: 'When I call you, you must take your wife by the hand and come into my office.' One day he called me to bring my wife. I went in the kitchen, and said, 'Mother, Mr. Griffith says you must come along with me to the office.' She stroked

her apron, and we went, and found the office full of
gentlemen, and there we stood as if we were just married." After answering some questions they went
back to their work, and their certificate of freedom was
recorded in the clerk's office in Burlington. They were
then hired at ten dollars a month. Quamino was
then forty-four years old. When asked by some of
his old friends, if he was happier since he received his
freedom, he said, " I don't know much about freedom,
but I would'nt be a slave again if you'd give me the
best farm in the Jarsies."

In the year 1842, when he was eighty years old,
his wife died suddenly. As the remains of Sarah
were borne from their humble home, he stood at the
door, supported by his crutches, the tears streaming
down his cheeks. " Farewell," said he, " I shall see
her no more, till we meet within the Pearl Gates."
Sarah was not inferior to her husband, to whom she
was a helper in spiritual and temporal things. He
felt this bereavement keenly, his situation without her
was forlorn. Living alone in his house, too feeble to
dress himself, his son, who was out at service, would
put him to bed at night, and come in the morning to
dress him. Arrangements were made by several
families to furnish him with dinner, each taking a
particular day; and this plan was pursued for eight
years. His landlord supplied his morning and evening meal, until Quamino's sight entirely failed, when
a faithful care-taker was provided for him.

Charles Taber, a Friend and a Minister, from Canada,

visited him one morning, and was fervently engaged
in prayer. When he rose from his knees Quamino
exclaimed, " Now I know that my prayer was heard.
Dis morning, after blessing and praising de Master
for taking care of me through de night, I asked Him
to please to send me something to comfort me through
the day, and now He sent you to me, oh, my dear
friend ! "

Speaking of the evidence of evil around us, he said,
"God is His own interpreter and my comforter, and
He will make all things plain." Referring to his
pains, he said, " The Lord is the physician—He has
a balm for every wound. It seems, as I sit here, I
have a view over Jordan. We must pass Jordan's
swelling flood, and then we'll be in the promised
land."

In reference to his blindness, he said, that with
his natural sight and comprehension he had never
been able to conceive the half of the glory which
should be revealed, or to form a conception of the
" good things " held in store even for so poor a creature as he felt himself to be. " How long I have to
remain in this state," he exclaimed, "the Lord
knows. I resign myself in His hands, and to His
wisdom. Oh, the Lord moves with me so beautiful !
I trust the Lord has enabled me to seek and to find
His face and favor."

Being inquired of concerning his health, he replied,
"That he could not wish to be better—that he was
so composed in mind, so calm and peaceable. Oh,

the glorious prospect I have in view. I can't see
anything of this world, but there seems to be a hovering around me. If the heart is composed to His
will, what can trouble us? Blessed Master, please
to give me an insight into Thy will." He spoke of
the comfort and strength which is afforded him to
hear the Holy Scriptures read.

"Oh," said he, "if I could only find words to express the feelings I have when I am alone—and yet
I do not feel that I am alone either. He cares for
us and provides for us; but He is all in all, and over
all; He leads us by His spirit; He don't compel us,
but enables us. Oh, my blessed Saviour, teach me,
oh, teach me the measure of my days, that I may turn
my thoughts more to it. But I trust in the Lord
that He will prepare me and keep me to the end."

Wm. J. Allinson called on him one morning. He
found the old man, who was 108 years of age, sitting
in his chair; he gave his visitor an earnest welcome,
and his tongue was eloquent with rejoicing praises
of Him who had made him meet for an inheritance
with the saints in light. "Glory be to my blessed
Master," he cried again and again, clasping his hands
like an artless and overjoyed child. On this occasion,
and indeed in almost every interview, he devoutly expressed his thankfulness that, although deprived of
sight, his reason and memory were spared him; and
this was remarkably the case to the last moment of
existence.

"My dear friend has been to visit me once more,"

he exclaimed repeatedly after this parting. This was his last conversation with any one, except a few words to his son and his attendant. In the night he called his son, and with his mental powers apparently clear to the last, and conscious that his end had arrived, his purified and enfranchised spirit deserted the clay tenement; and who can doubt his welcome into the joy of the Lord?

A few weeks afterwards a sermon relating to Quamino was preached by the pastor of the Methodist congregation to which this aged Christian belonged. The text was, "This poor man cried, and the Lord heard him, and delivered him out of all his troubles." Psalm xxxiv. 6.

> "See thy Saviour bending o'er thee,
>   Even to old age the same,
> Set life's one chief end before thee,
>   Still to glorify its name ;
> While on Himself is fixed thy sight,
> At evening-time there shall be light."

EMANCIPATION IN NEW YORK.

THE period fixed by law for the termination of slavery in the State of New York was the 4th of July, 1827. According to the census of 1820, there were 20,279 free persons of color, and 10,092 slaves in the State ; making in all 30,371.

THE FREEDMEN OF AMERICA.

DURING the four years' war commencing 1861 the colored people fled from bondage, and gathered in large numbers around Washington, and in those parts of Virginia which were in possession of the United States Government. Sometimes one thousand refugees came to the freedmen's settlement in a week, and most of them had travelled on foot for several days, with scant food and clothing. They rejoiced greatly when they arrived at a place of refuge, and became free men and women. The able-bodied men were employed by the Government, but the sick and aged, the women and children, were cared for by different benevolent associations of the churches at the North and West. The Religious Society of Friends always cherished a deep feeling for the enslaved people of color, and after sending agents to ascertain the condition of the freedmen in the camps and quarters assigned to them by the Government, they earnestly labored to feed, clothe and teach those for whom they had long solicited the boon of freedom.

Believing some incidents and anecdotes from letters received from the agents of Friends will be interesting to many, the following extracts are presented :

" It is difficult to make a connected account of our visit among the freedmen at Washington and elsewhere. We went into their cabins, the tents, and the hospitals, looking into the condition of the poor people congregated there. Their stories may be considered almost trifling in themselves, and yet summed up as a whole—a people's history—they tell the oft-repeated tale of sorrow, degradation, and oppression in slavery; of hunger and cold, of sickness and suffering, patiently and uncomplainingly borne, in their great struggle for freedom. Every sacrifice, every privation seems insignificant compared to the blessed boon of liberty, to them and to their children. ' The good Lord Jesus has at last heard our prayers and sent Uncle Abram to set us free.'

" They come to the Union as little children would to a parent, with perfect confidence that they will be helped. The younger women mostly had their children with them, but the older ones had all come off ' wid 'lations and friends.' In a severe snow-storm one thousand arrived, with only the clothes on their backs. Their utter poverty is terrible. During this storm we had not clothes for the children, who were crying to get out of bed. Nine hundred came yesterday—all ragged ; their masters had not given them clothes, some for a year, others for two years. All beg for Bibles."

" The rope-walk is a very long building divided into cabins; it is where the refugees come at first. In each cabin live four or five families. It is the most interesting place to visit. There are over five hundred people there, fresh from slave-life, and re-

joicing over their freedom.   Not being able to read,
they often burst out as we are reading to them with,
' Well, I never heard that before.'

" The beautiful doctrine of the golden rule seems
almost new to them.   It is true the religious element
is very strong in them, but their manner of receiving
it is very different from our ideas.   Although they
may be what they call converted, they need plain
words of moral truth for every-day life.   They have
plenty of faith and thankfulness, but not Christ's law
of love in their hearts to govern every action.

" We stopped at a church and witnessed one of
their religious excitements—women all rocking their
bodies and singing weird choruses ; then some one getting excited above the others, and throwing herself
about, jumping and screaming.   We stayed until
they were out, and all down the aisles they sang and
shouted—real fine, full voices, and the words more
strange than all.   All the women had that swaying
motion so peculiar to them.

" The boxes were handed over to me on the 19th
of January.   From that date to the 7th of May, I
have given out twenty-six hundred and twenty garments, large and small.   For the last ten days we
have been very busy.   During the last engagement
on the battle-field, hundreds have come, more than
can possibly find shelter here.   I have witnessed some
of the arrivals at the depôt.   At the sound of the
whistle, many anxious hearts and longing eyes are
seeking their friends.   Here mothers find their long-

lost children. Husbands and wives, brothers and sisters, meet after long separation. One good old mother here found six of her children in one group. One poor mother, with seven children, was inquiring for her husband: the answer was, 'he is dead!' The small-pox left that record for this poor mother.

"We saw one noble-looking man, not far from seven feet high, in mere rags and bare feet. Our No. 12's looked like baby-shoes beside them; but I heard of a pair of No. 19 at the Commissary, which they were very glad to exchange. The old man had had a hard master, and had been driven off 'without food enough to cover a pin.' But I never saw such a flash of joy as when I said, 'But, uncle, you have such a *good*, *kind* master now, and such a beautiful home up in heaven.' 'Oh, missis, it's *that*, it's jest *that*, that's 'stained me all along.' They all seemed so grateful, and we had a happy day indeed."

"They learn surprisingly fast; they were very anxious to learn to reckon. I said I would repeat the multiplication table if they would try to remember it. I repeated the 2's once, and they said it after me in concert. I then questioned them, and though they had never heard it before, quite a number remembered the whole.

"One little fellow in the school being asked if he knew his letters, said, promptly, 'Yes, ma'am.'

" Well, what else do you know ?

" Drawing himself up to his full height, which might
be about four feet, he replied, ' I know a 'heap.' "

" Freedman's Village, near Arlington, is really an
attractive-looking place; comfortable houses, nicely
white-washed; a school-house, capable of accommo-
dating two or three hundred children, and a ' Home '
for the aged and infirm. Fervor and earnestness per-
vade the sermons and prayers of the colored people
here.   One gave thanks for ' the glorious privilege
that we ain't all dead and shut up in hell.'

" Some of us might not have realized before that it
was a glorious privilege to be still left on earth, either
as faithful servants, to do the Master's bidding, or to
become reconciled to Him before we were snatched
away with no alternative but to be ' shut up in hell.'

" You would have been touched to witness their
grief at the death of our beloved President.   Every
tenanted hut was decked with some badge of mourn-
ing.   Thousands went to look at their emancipator,
as he lay in state in the White House.   Aunt Cicily,
who bore the yoke of slavery one hundred and ten
years, looked on Mr. Lincoln with a reverential feeling, beautiful to behold in one so aged—' for the
privilege,' she says, ' that he gave me to die free.' "

" Some old men who had learned to read while in
slavery, said, ' We toted massa's children to school,
stayed all day, and then toted them back. We learned
to read, and massa didn't know it; and now we can
read de blessed Book ourselves. De good people of
de North have been bery good, bery good to us.
Jesus tell dem to help de poor slave : by-and-by we
can help ourselves. We tank you all bery much !'
Mother, child, and grandchild sometimes go hand-in-
hand to the school-room. The stimulating motive
with most of the adults is a fervent desire to read the
Bible."

" The marriage record kept among the Freedmen,
shows that a large part of the marriages, especially at
first, were of those who had lived together as husband
and wife, perhaps many years, without an opportunity to be legally united. One old man, of almost
three-score and ten, was thus joined in lawful marriage to his venerable wife. At the conclusion of the
ceremony, when the pastor extended his hand with
the nuptial benediction, and dismissed them with a
short prayer, they dropped on their knees together,
their eyes streaming with tears of thankfulness, and
still kneeling, the old man reached out both arms and
hugged her to his heart, saying aloud, ' My dear old
woman, I bless God that I can now, for the first time,
kiss my own lawful wife.' "

An agent, under date 5th month, 1863, writes:

"When I first wrote to thee, the supply of excellent clothing, furnished by New York Friends, and other quarters, seemed so ample that, to my eyes, the subject of further need, did not suggest itself. I thought the time must come when such wants must be satisfied. But that time dawns not yet. The hospitals for colored people are a heavy drain on the clothing. Now, that the army advances, there are daily arrivals of freedmen; they come with only the clothing they have on, and must have a change to preserve health.

LETTERS FROM A LADY AGENT IN RICHMOND, 1866.

"In my jaunt to Deep Creek, and to the poor cabins in Dismal Swamp, I helped mend six bridges before our horse could cross, borrowing rails from the fence. It was a very hard trip—no chance for a single dinner while gone—but it paid. The same night I mended bridges, I found work of a different kind. Going on business to the Bute Street Church, I found a love-feast under full headway: about two hundred were present; the excitement terrible among the young converts, who, in their frantic leaps, broke lamps and windows, and filled the house with perfect uproar. I found the new pastor dared not risk his popularity by checking it. Courage was given me to make my way to the pulpit, when I at once had permission to speak. All was still as need be, while I appealed to their judgment, and the teachings of the Bible. I saw I had the sympathy of most, and when at last, I said, 'wait till the wind, and the earthquake, and the fire have all passed by, and then go to your homes and listen to the still small voice by which God himself will teach you; and oh, remember, my young sisters, that the proof of your growth in grace is not the *feelings* you have here to-night, but the *life* you will lead to-morrow.' There was such an earnest 'amen,' all over the house, as gave me hope again that they will rise above this great delusion. Many came to thank me. 'It was just what we needed, and they will hear it from you.'"

"Deeply impressed with the moral wants of these poor creatures, especially the women, and their need of friendly counsel in their new position, I have opened Mother's meetings—now held weekly, in each of our three-school districts—where they are invited to come with their work and their babies. I talk familiarly with them about their household matters, the cheapest and most wholesome food, the best ways of cooking it, and the right care of their children, and their duties to their husbands—often being greatly helped out in my own stock of knowledge by the practical experience of some nice old aunty, who tells how she manages, till the whole group is at ease and can confide their troubles and trials. Then I read, teach, or talk to them. Finally, all lay aside their work, and the babies are hushed up, while they listen to a chapter from the Bible; and the devotional pause at the close is solemn and impressive. Those who cannot spare two or three hours, hurry in at the last, and I hear them saying 'I'se just goin' over to prayers, 'pears like it gives me *such* a lift.'"

LOVE FOR THE BIBLE.

AT a great fire in the city of New York a hundred houses had been burned. Dr. Ely overtook a colored woman who was carrying under one arm a bundle of wood, and under the other a large Bible.

"Poor woman," said he, "have you been burnt out too?" "Yes, sir," said she, "but blessed be God, I'm alive." "You are very old to be turned out of house and home." "I'm well stricken in years, but God does it." "Have you saved nothing but the Bible?" "Nothing," said she, "but one trunk of things; but this blessed Book is worth more than all the rest; it makes me feel better than all the rest. So long as I keep this, I am content."

HYMN.

SUNG AT CHRISTMAS BY THE SCHOLARS AT ST. HELENA'S
ISLAND, S. C.

O NONE in all the world before
  Were ever glad as we !
We're free on Carolina's shore,
  We're all at home and free.

Thou Friend and Helper of the poor,
  Who suffered for our sake,
To open every prison door,
  And every yoke to break,

Bend low Thy pitying face and mild,
  And help us sing and pray;
The hand that blessed the little child,
  Upon our foreheads lay.

We hear no more the driver's horn,
  No more the whip we fear;
This holy day that saw Thee born,
  Was never half so dear.

The very oaks are greener clad,
  The waters brighter smile ;
O never shone a day so glad
  On sweet St. Helen's isle.

We praise Thee in our songs to-day,
  To Thee in prayer we call ;
Make swift the feet and straight the way,
  Of freedom unto all.

Come once again, O blessed Lord!
Come walking on the sea!
And let the main-lands hear the word
That sets the islands free.

                                    J. G. WHITTIER.

A TEMPERANCE MEETING IN AFRICA.

JAMES BACKHOUSE, an English Friend and a minister, published a journal of his mission in Africa, in
which he says, under date of December 1st, 1838—

This is the memorable day in which slavery ceased
in Cape Colony, South Africa. We arrived at Han-
key in time to join a considerable congregation of
those who had been in bondage—natives of Mada-
gascar and Mozambique, as well as home-born slaves;
they had come from the surrounding country to unite
with those on the mission station in praising God for
their deliverance from bondage. In the evening a
meeting was held, when several Hottentots (natives of
South Africa) and freedmen addressed the congregation. The next day was "a Sabbath day," and truly
"a high day." About five hundred freed slaves and
Hottentots assembled early in the morning; they held
a prayer-meeting, in which the language of thanksgiving was held forth by one lately in slavery, and appropriate hymns were sung. I exhorted the liberated to
seek, through Jesus Christ, deliverance from that

worst of bondage—slavery to sin.   In the evening of
the third day a temperance tea-meeting was held in
the chapel.   A suspended wheel-tire was struck for a
bell, to call them to assemble.   The men sat at the
tables on one side of the chapel, and the women at
the other side; tea and cakes were dealt out by some
of the women.   All were remarkably clean, and conducted themselves with sober cheerfulness and looks
full of interest.   After the Missionary had returned
thanks and made a brief address, it was my privilege
to follow him in recommending total abstinence from
intoxicating liquors.   Several Hottentots and freed
slaves then addressed the meeting, which afterwards
adjourned for a short interval at milking time.   On
re-assembling, George W. Walker spoke at some length,
and several others.

At half-past ten the Missionary suggested that it
would be unseasonable to continue the meeting longer;
he therefore opened a book of signatures to the total-
abstinence pledge, and one hundred and sixty new
names were received.   As neither my companion, G.
W. Walker, nor I had hitherto signed such a pledge,
we also added our names.   A sweet sense of the love
of God overshadowed this meeting.

Some attention had been paid to temperance from
the early institution of this settlement.   The children
have so little idea of what drunkenness is, that in
1842, when an Englishman appeared in a state of intoxication, some of them ran away, thinking he was
mad; others thought he must be ill because he stag-

gered, but others feared he was blind, and offered to lead him.

At the expiration of a year from this period, only one of the persons who signed the pledge on this day, was known to have broken it, and that only to the amount of taking a single glass of wine.

LIBERTY TO THE CAPTIVE.

WRITTEN ON THE ANNIVERSARY OF BRITISH EMANCI-
PATION.

> On, Holy Father ! just and true
>   Are all thy works, and words, and ways;
> And unto Thee alone are due
>   Thanksgiving and eternal praise !
> As children of Thy gracious care,
>   We veil the eye—we bend the knee ;
> With broken words of praise and prayer,
>   Father and God, we come to Thee.
>
> For Thou hast heard, O God of Right !
>   The sighing of the island slave,
> And stretched for him the arm of might,
>   Not shortened that it could not save.
> The laborer sits beneath his vine,
>   The shackled soul and hand are free—
> Thanksgiving !—for the work is Thine !
> Praise !—for the blessing is of Thee !

WHITTIER.

www.ingramcontent.com/pod-product-compliance
Lightning Source LLC
Chambersburg PA
CBHW031333070726
47496CB00018B/1843